VALHALLA ONLINE

A RAGNAROK SAGA LITRPG ADVENTURE

KEVIN MCLAUGHLIN

ROLE OF THE HERO PUBLISHING

Second Edition

Copyright © 2017, 2018 by Kevin O. McLaughlin

All rights reserved.

No part of this book may be reproduced in any form or by any electronic or mechanical means, including information storage and retrieval systems, without written permission from the author, except for the use of brief quotations in a book review.

This is a work of fiction. Any resemblance to actual persons living or dead, businesses, events, or locales is purely coincidental.

1

Samantha woke with a groggy feeling. No, it was worse than that. This felt more like a five-alarm hangover. Shit, what had she been drinking? She had to get up and be ready for PT by eight, and then duty until god-damned five o'clock. It was going to be a long f-ing day.

She reached over to slap the obnoxious ringing of her phone alarm and check the time. Maybe she could snooze another eight minutes. Her hand passed right through where the phone should have rested on her night-stand, hitting nothing but air.

Bolting upright in an instant and regretting it, Sam peeled her burning eyelids open and looked around.

"What the hell?" she said. Her head was still pounding in time with the banging of some sort of alarm. It sounded like a gong? Who was beating a gong?

It wasn't until her eyes were open that Sam became aware something was terribly, horribly wrong. Either she was in the middle of the most f-ed up nightmare she'd ever had, or... The thought trailed off. She didn't have another good answer.

She wasn't in her bed. Or her room. Or her cute cubby of an apartment in the junior officer barracks at Fort Drum. Sam wasn't sure where she was, but she very clearly was *not* in the proverbial Kansas anymore!

The bed she was laying on was a mattress of rough cloth over a frame made of heavy sticks. Whatever the mattress was stuffed with didn't feel very comfortable either. Bits of it stuck up through the cloth and stabbed her skin. The sheet covering her was more of the same thick cloth as the mattress.

It looked a little like a bed she might have imagined a prisoner slept on. If the prisoner were living in another century, or some Third World country.

The room was just as strange. All the walls were made of stone, the floor and ceiling too. Heavy timbers were spaced about the walls, which supported more beams that crisscrossed the ceiling. The room wasn't large, but had a dozen beds in it. She'd been in enough barracks rooms to recognize the look.

That gong was going to drive her crazy if they didn't knock it off. Her headache was beginning to fade, but it was hard to think. Sam went back over what she could last recall, trying to figure out how she'd gotten from there to here. Wherever here was.

She'd pulled a double shift yesterday. There was a missing man investigation she was involved in. Except it hadn't just been one person missing. There were three recent disappearances, and Sam's gut said there was a link connecting them. It was a slim lead, but enough that she'd started doing some snooping around the base. She remembered driving her car. She was supposed to be meeting someone, but for the life of her she couldn't remember who.

Her brain was usually sharp as a tack. Why was she having such a hard time remembering things? She could recall what she had for breakfast the morning before: two hard-boiled eggs, toast, three strips of bacon, all chowed down in the First Brigade dining facility after PT. She thought their DFAC served the best food on base, and as an MP she had a little more freedom to move around than most grunts would.

But everything after that was hazy, and the later in the day the less clear her memory became. Had she been drugged? Hauled off somewhere?

Sam took stock of her situation. She wasn't tied down. There were no handcuffs, and she didn't seem to be injured. There was a strange looking little dot in the lower left corner of her vision, though. She glanced at it, and it lit up.

Without warning an apparition of a woman appeared at the foot of her bed. Her outfit was almost as uncanny as her sudden appearance. She was wearing some sort of linked ring armor, and what looked like a steel medieval helmet on her head. To top it off she was holding a six foot spear in her right hand.

Sam scuttled away from the woman, or whatever she was. At first she was backing away from the crazy person holding the weapon, but the woman didn't move toward her in a threatening manner. She just stood there smiling.

People did *not* just appear out of thin air. More sure than ever she was having a dream, she wanted some answers anyway.

"Who the hell are you?" Sam asked.

"I am your Tutorial Guide!" the woman said with a cheerful smile. "You may call me Helga."

"Helga, where the hell am I?"

"You are in Valhalla Online, the final resting place of the deserving. Where those who earned honor in life get to carry on in battle, mead, and song for all eternity through the magic of modern technology," Helga said.

It sounded like a corporate spiel. She did catch the word 'online' though. Suddenly everything made a little more sense.

"I'm gonna kill Jeff, when I get my fingers around his neck," Sam said. She waved her arm around the room. "None of this is real, is it?"

"You're correct. Everything you see is a virtual representation. Lines of code, brought to life for you," Helga said. "Everything will feel, taste, and sound just like the real thing."

Definitely had to be Jeff. Captain Jeffrey Hunter was a computer geek who worked in Brigade headquarters, doing classified stuff of the sort that he joked about having to shoot anyone he told about. He'd bragged to her about this gadget he'd bought, a full immersion virtual reality suit. You put on the suit, connect to the 'Net, and bang! There you were, in some alternate reality. Except it was all a game, a fake reality where nerds hung out and beat on each other because they didn't have a life.

That was Sam's take on things, anyway. Jeff had seemed more than a little hurt when she'd told him as much. Her gut said this was his way of getting back at her. Somehow he'd hooked her up to his machine and plunked her into this world. She'd tear his head off when she got out.

"OK, Jeff. Let me out. NOW!" Sam said to the air.

There wasn't any answer. Fine. Let him have his fun, for now. She'd figure out how to log off herself, and then she'd flay him alive. This was not cool. She might be the new kid on base, but he had no right to do this to her without her permission.

A niggling voice in the back of her head suggested that it might not be Jeff. That with that suit tech, anyone could kidnap any person they wanted and potentially lock them into a world for as long as they desired. She shoved away the thought as paranoid. It had to be Jeff. Occam's razor said the most likely solution was probably the correct one.

"Helga, how do I log off?" she asked.

"I'm sorry, I don't have an answer for that question," Helga responded.

"How do I leave the game?" she said, trying different words.

"I'm sorry, I don't have an answer for that question," the guide repeated.

Sam frowned. That seemed to be some sort of stock answer. Basic code that covered any situation that it wasn't programmed to handle. Why was getting out of the game not covered under basic help? Shouldn't that be one of the most important things to know?

The voice in the back of her head tried to rear up again, warning her that this could be anyone, and she could be anywhere. She shoved it down again. It took a little more effort this time.

"Congratulations!" Helga said. "You've arrived in the middle of an Epic Battle!"

Sam could almost hear the capital letters around *Epic Battle*. "Are those the alarms I am hearing?"

"Yes! The keep is under attack. The enemy will attempt to scale the walls, slay everyone inside, and tear your team's banner down from the highest tower," Helga said. "Your mission is to prevent this."

"My mission is to get the hell out of this stupid game,"

Sam growled. She didn't have time for this bullshit. But Helga kept smiling, ignoring her words.

"You will need this gift to help you defend the keep," Helga said, handing her the spear she carried. Sam took it carefully. The haft was longer than she was tall, and there was a leaf-bladed tip placed on one end, about the size of her hand.

The last thing she wanted was to play ball here. She stood up from the bed to set the spear against the wall beside her, which gave her a first good look at herself. The clothing made her growl again. She wasn't wearing much. A leather halter covered her breasts, and tight cloth shorts made of some moderately translucent cloth clad her legs down to a few inches above her knees. Her feet were bare. Someone was definitely going to pay for this.

"I want out. Now!" Sam yelled at the guide.

"To go out, exit this door. You can climb up the stairs to the ramparts, or down to enter the courtyard," Helga said. "Can I assist you any further?"

"No," Sam said. "You haven't helped me at all."

"Good luck!" Helga said, still beaming the same fixed smile. Then she vanished the same way she had appeared.

"God damn..." Sam started to say. Before she could start swearing a blue streak, there was a commotion from outside the door Helga had pointed to. She froze, keeping quiet out of instinct. The noise grew louder, a clash of steel on steel. There were grunts and a cry of pain. Then silence.

Sam remained as motionless as possible. A trickle of sweat ran down her forehead, the small reminder of reality in stark contrast to the idea that this was some sort of game.

The door swung inward with a crash. Two men walked in. They were big. Each was at least six feet tall. Both had beards and long dark hair. Each of them wore heavy leather over their torsos. One had a spear, and the other was carrying a sword. They both looked across at her and sneered. Spear guy's sneer had an edge that Sam particularly didn't care for. Her fingers twitched toward her own spear out of reflex.

"Newb," the man with the sword said. "Want to leave her be?"

"Easy XP," the spearman said, shrugging.

"Good point," the first man replied. "Sorry honey. This won't hurt too much."

Then the two men raised their weapons and began to advance across the floor toward Sam.

2

As the two men advanced on her, Sam took stock of her situation. The weapons they carried looked real enough. So did the blood dripping down their blades. She reminded herself again and again that this whole thing wasn't real. She was in a simulation. It was just a game. The way the guide had appeared and then vanished proved that, even if nothing else would.

The problem was it didn't feel like a game. She could smell something burning nearby, a little of the smoke wafting into the room now that the door was open. There was nothing artificial about the way the men advancing on her moved, or the grim look they both wore on their faces. She might know this wasn't real, but part of her brain was screaming at her that it was real enough to be afraid of those weapons.

"Guys, look. Can we talk about this?" she said.

"Not personal, honey, but we have to end you to win," the spearman said. "Don't worry. This won't hurt much."

"Look how scared she is. Newbie," the swordsman

chuckled. "Damn, girl. Dying ain't that bad. We're all dead in this place anyway."

Sam wasn't sure what he meant by that, but she wasn't going to sit around while they stuck steel into her. She reached over and snatched the spear from where she'd set it against the wall. The staff felt unfamiliar in her hand, but it wasn't the first time she'd used a long weapon. She'd done pretty well in the pugil stick pits at West Point.

That had been a couple of years ago, though. And those sticks hadn't been pointy. She took the spear in a two-handed grip with the point aimed in the direction of the men.

"Oh, the pup is trying to bare fangs, huh?" the spearman said.

"Flank her," the swordsman said. "This is already more work than she's worth for XP. Let's finish this."

The two men split up, coming at her from opposite sides. Sam tried to adjust her position to prevent being surrounded, but the room was too large, and she was too far from a corner to make it into one. She jabbed out with the spear to keep the swordsman away. He chuckled in response. Her spear hadn't come closer than a couple of feet from his body.

Sam sensed more than heard the spearman move, and shifted the pole of her spear just in time to block a stab. Her block saved her, sending the spear tip grazing across her back instead of sliding into her abdomen. The pain was real enough...but less severe than she'd expected. She knew that the blade had cut deep enough to cause drips of blood to well up across her lower back, but it felt more like a cat scratch than a serious blow.

"See, it won't even hurt much," the swordsman crooned to her. "We'll make it quick."

"Like hell," she growled. She was tired of playing defensive games. That wasn't going to help her. Game or not, there was a part of Sam that wanted to be the best. At pretty much anything she did. That drive had gotten her into West Point, had carried her from there into her career beyond. Whether or not she wanted to be in this stupid game, a couple of smug assholes were not going to get the better of her without feeling it.

She whirled back on the swordsman, lashing out with her spear. Rather than stabbing, this time she used the blade like the tip of a long knife. It raked across at his head height. He blocked with his sword, but he was nowhere near as good with his weapon as he seemed to think he was. She whipped the spear back from where he'd blocked it and thrust it in toward his gut.

The leather chest plate he wore blocked a lot of the blow, but she could tell the tip had gone in at least a little. The swordsman staggered back, his free hand covering the spot she'd stabbed.

Sam had only a moment to feel satisfaction before a sharp pain flashed in her leg. It felt like the worst muscle cramp ever. Not a blinding pain, but intense enough that she winced as she looked down.

The spearman had used her moment of distraction to stab her leg with his own weapon. He withdrew the spear head from her leg. The feeling of the steel leaving her body as she watched, of feeling blood drip down freely from her leg, was dizzying. For a moment her body reacted to the wound as it would to a real blow, and she felt like she wanted to throw up, or curl herself on the floor around the wound. Maybe both.

With an effort she focused on remembering that this was all a game. The wound was not real. The body she was playing in here was not real. This was a make-believe computer generated illusion. Even if it did hurt.

"Bitch. We were going to make it easy for you," the swordsman said, wincing and clutching at his wound. She must have hit him harder than she'd thought. "Now we're going to kill you slow."

Sam swung her spear in an arc, trying to keep both of the men at bay. There was no way to attack one without the other immediately closing on her, and they knew it as well as she did. In another minute they would rush her, and she'd feel their steel. Again. She wondered what dying would be like in this game. Her leg and back still throbbed from the injuries she'd sustained. She had a feeling this wasn't going to be fun.

"Or you could pick on someone your own size," drawled a voice from the doorway.

He was an old man with snow white hair and a white beard that looked like it might once have been red. He was short, only an inch or two taller than Sam's five foot six. But his shoulders were broad, stocky, and well-muscled. He also seemed to have a lot more armor than the men Sam was facing. He wore a shirt made of connected rings of steel, a lot like the one the Helga-guide had worn. His legs and arms were also armored with thick blue-dyed leather reinforced with strips of steel. He was carrying both a hand axe and a shield.

"We can arrange that," the swordsman said. He sounded decidedly more nervous now than he had a moment before, though. He stepped back a bit from Sam, his attention clearly on the bigger, better armored threat in the room. The spearman also backed away from her to approach the newcomer, leaving Sam more or less to her own devices.

She tried to take a few steps toward them, but her leg

didn't want to work right. She staggered a step or two and then almost fell to the floor. Fat lot of good she was going to be to her rescuer if she couldn't even walk.

The two aggressors closed on the old man rapidly. The spearman stabbed in. The old man swung his shield across his body to block the shot, knocking the spearhead off to the side. The swordsman took advantage of his shield being out of alignment to swing down at the man's shoulder. His sword glanced from the steel rings, but the old man's face showed that some of the impact had gone through.

He swung the shield like a weapon, bashing the swordsman in the face. The top edge of the shield splintered with the impact with a crunching sound that didn't sound like it was entirely from the wood breaking. Before the man could recover from the stunning blow to the face, the old man swung his axe in low, cutting a deep gash into the inside of the swordsman's thigh. Blood fountained from the wound, and he crumpled to the floor, holding his leg.

The spearman was still in the fight, though. He'd drawn the spear back, and was preparing for a mighty stab into the old man's undefended flank. Sam didn't know whether the ring armor would block such a blow or not, but the old man was risking his neck to help her. She wasn't just going to stand there.

There was no way she could close the gap in time. But a spear was meant to be thrown, right? She hefted the weapon overhand and tossed it toward the enemy spearman's back.

She missed his back. Her throw almost missed him altogether, but the spear struck the back of his calf, stabbing in a few inches before tearing itself out and clattering to the ground. The man cried out in surprise and hurt. Clearly, he'd forgotten her in his focus on taking down the greater threat.

Staggered by the new wound, his own thrust was off target and missed the old man entirely. The axeman grinned wolfishly at the spearman and closed quickly.

The spearman tried to back away, stabbing almost blindly to keep the old man at bay. He batted aside the strike with his shield and then rushed in close, hacking away with his axe. Three strikes later, the spearman lay dead at his feet. With practiced ease, he went to the other man's body, still laying curled on the floor. One blow ended the swordsman's life as well.

Only then did he turn that wolf-like grin on Sam.

3

He stood there staring at her for a moment, then looked down at the spear she'd cast, where it lay on the ground. He picked the thing up, examining it and nodding to himself.

"Not completely useless then, are you?" he said.

"It's been a long time since I threw javelins in track and field," Sam replied. "Thank you. I was in real trouble there."

"We're all in real trouble right now," he replied. "I can't believe they sent a new spirit in here, right at this time... The Greens are making their big push right now. You're stuck in the middle of it."

"Greens? Push? I don't have the foggiest idea what you're talking about," she said.

"Of course you don't. Worst of it is, I don't have time to explain it all to you right now," he said. "After the fight, sure. Now hold still."

He went to the bedside and tore big strips of cloth from the blanket. Then he stepped to her side and knelt down, carefully tying the strips around her leg wound. The wound felt better almost immediately.

"Thanks," she said.

"No problem. You're no use to us immobile. I've taught you the Wound Care skill, so you can bind your own wounds next time," he said.

"Taught me what?" she asked, confused.

"Icon, lower right of your view. Look at it," he grunted, standing back up.

She hadn't noticed the icon there while the fight was going on, but it was definitely there now. She looked at it, and it expanded into a translucent bubble with words inside.

Congratulations! You have learned the skill 'Spear'! The pointy end goes in the other guy!

Congratulations! You have learned the skill 'Wound Care'! The life you save...might be your own!

Sam groaned a little at the puns. But it was good to have an idea what she could do. "I'm going to guess I don't start out with a lot of skills?" she asked.

"Gotta earn them, girl. Mostly the hard way, unless you find someone willing to teach them," he replied. "I'm Harald. You up for coming with me and helping defend this place? I won't blame you if you decide to hide in here and sit this one out, being as new as you are."

Sam had the feeling from his tone that he would absolutely think less of her if she didn't go with him. Part of her argued that she ought to just stay put. This stupid game wasn't her thing. She had no intention of playing along with Jeff, or whoever had put her in here.

But at the same time there was a part of her that wanted to rise to this challenge. Something about the way Harald canted his head, grinning through his beard with his white hair flopping around like a madman's halo made her like the guy. She wanted him to think well of her. He had rescued her, after all. She could return the favor and play along with the game for a bit.

"I'm Samantha. Call me Sam," she said. "Tell me what I need to do to help."

He grunted, seeming satisfied. "First off, grab the leather top off the asshole with the spear. It's still in good enough shape that it will give you more protection than that...whatever it is you're wearing."

Sam blushed as she glanced down at herself again. She wasn't used to parading around in what was basically a leather bikini top. The sight brought her ire back to the surface again. The idea of stripping clothes off the dead didn't really appeal to her either. She gingerly touched the still form at first, but then reminded herself that it wasn't like the guy was actually dead. Even now he was likely respawning someplace. This was all just pixels.

Sometimes it was hard to remember that. Like when her hand slipped on the warm blood pooling under the body, and she had to wipe the stuff off on the tunic he wore. It felt god-damned real.

The leather chest piece was thick, a lot heavier than coat or even boot leather. It was like a vest that laced under the arms instead of in front. That made sense. If you were hoping to stop attacks with blades, then you didn't want a gap over your guts. She threw the thing over her shoulders and laced it up quickly. Harald was already at the door, peering outward for more enemies.

"They've taken the west wall with a good sized force," he said.

"How do you know?" Sam asked.

"I can hear the fighting," Harald said. "When you've defended this old beast as many times as I have, you get a feel for how the battles flow. We're losing this one."

"What happens if we lose?" she asked.

"They kill all of us," he replied with a toothy smile. "I'd rather not."

"What can we do?"

"You ready? Then follow me," he replied before darting out into the hall.

She followed, leaving the barracks room for a stonework corridor, dimly lit by thin windows. A breeze flowed through those gaps along with the sunlight, smelling of smoke and iron. Sam shivered. She told herself it was the cold floor on her bare feet, and not the certainty that the iron smell was from spilled blood.

They passed more several more dead bodies as they jogged down the passage. Harald stopped next to a pair of them, dropping his broken shield to the floor and snatching up an unbroken defense from one of the bodies. There was another shield there on the floor. He picked that up as well and handed it to Sam.

"They don't last long, but it might keep you alive a little longer," he said.

The shield had a center-grip bar tucked inside a small steel cap in the middle. She grabbed the bar and held it as tightly as she could.

"No," Harald said. "Relax the grip. Let it pivot freely in your hand and…Odin's name, girl, you'd best be worth all this time and trouble on the battlefield."

He paused, reaching over to touch her forearm. An icon sprung up in her vision again. When she glanced at it, words appeared again.

Congratulations! You have learned the skill 'Shield'! Sometimes the best offense is a good defense!

Somehow she knew that her grip was wrong and how to fix it without being told more. She loosened her hold on the shield, allowing the grip to move a little more freely between her fingers. It still felt like an ungainly weight on her arm, but she had a sense that she would be able to block at least some attacks with the thing.

It was a strange feeling, to have knowledge appear in her mind like that. To even have reflexes arrive without having to build them up. She supposed that was just how games like this worked. When you learned a skill, the knowledge to use the skill was loaded onto your profile. Sam wondered if any of that would stick with her once she got the hell out of this place.

"How did you do that?" she asked.

"I've mastered the Shield skill. Any master can train others in a skill," he replied. "Now follow close. When we get out there, stick mostly to shield work. Keep the enemy from flanking me and leave the killing to my axe."

Sam nodded. She could feel her pulse quickening as they started down the hall again. Adrenaline surged through her body. Or her mind. Or something...whatever the equivalent was in this unreal place. Her lizard brain couldn't tell the difference between this and a real battle. Sam was beginning to understand why people might be attracted to this sort of rush. It was all of the heat of battle without the real risk of dying.

Harald was moving at a light jog by the time they reached the end of the hall, where a heavy wooden door blocked their way. A bar had blocked the door from their side, but it lay cracked and broken on the stone floor. Harald put his hand on an iron ring set into the door and then looked back at her.

"You ready? Gonna be fast and furious when we get out there," he said.

"I've got your back," Sam replied. She'd been through

military training in the real world. Surely she could handle some fake medieval battle. Right?

He made a huffing noise under his breath, but Harald seemed satisfied. He pulled the door inward and stepped into the sunlight beyond. Sam hesitated only a moment before following him.

4

The daylight was blinding after the dimly lit interior. The cacophony of the battle raging around them was nearly deafening. Samantha wanted to cover her ears with her hands, but they were filled with spear and shield. They'd exited onto a rampart which ran across the top of a stone wall, complete with battlements. The battlements were on her left. Off to her right was a straight drop down into a courtyard twenty feet below. A fall might not kill her, but it would be bad.

The battle raged only a dozen feet ahead. Men with green bandanas tied to their arms, or with green paint on their shields, were holding a position on the wall facing off against a squad of blue-bearing troops.

The bad news was that the green troops — whom Sam assumed were the enemy — had ladders up against the outside of the wall. More troops were climbing into the fort every moment. The good news was that most of them were facing the blue troops on the other side of the rampart. Their backs were to Harald and Sam.

Harald didn't pause for more than a moment to let his eyes adjust before rushing in. He gave a terrific scream, bashing the one green warrior with his shield as he was trying to climb onto the wall. The man lost his balance and fell backwards outside the fort. There was a long cry as he fell, which cut off suddenly. It sounded like the drop on the other side of the wall was at least as far as the one on this side.

An arrow flashed upward from somewhere outside the fort. Acting entirely on instinct, Sam raised her shield just in time to ward the shot. It stuck into the wood with a resounding thunk. The impact stung her fingers and left them buzzing. How the hell had she found herself in this crazy situation? Last thing she knew she'd been on the beat with a nine mil pistol on her hip. She found herself wishing for the weapon. These assholes would see something then. She hadn't qualified expert with her sidearm the last three years in a row for nothing.

Sam didn't have time to wonder about the strangeness of defending a castle wall with a pointy stick. More green warriors were coming over the wall every moment. Harald didn't pay them any mind. He simply rushed into the rear of the formation already up on the wall. His axe began working its deadly way through their ranks.

That left the steady flow of reinforcements for Sam to deal with. She supposed that was what the old man had meant when he said her job was to make sure the enemy didn't flank him. There were three ladders though, which meant three warriors coming up at her!

She lashed out with her spear at the nearest to the top. He leaned back, avoiding her strike. But he lost his grip on the ladder trying to avoid the blow and tumbled away out of sight. Two more men were almost over the edge, though, and each ladder had more warriors panting with their effort to ascend as quickly as they could.

Sam struck another man as he clambered over the battlements. Her spear went into his side, and he fell to the stone rampart clutching the wound. There was a space now on two of the ladders, the leading climber a few feet down. She raced to the first, grabbed the top rung, and shoved.

It was heavy! The weight of half a dozen men pushed back against her. She heaved with everything she had. The nearest green fighter was only two feet below her now. She looked into his snarling face as he grabbed another rung, hauling himself up. He carried a wicked curved axe in his hand and the promise to use it on her in his eyes.

One last shove, and the ladder shifted, moved, and tumbled over backwards. The more fortunate warriors climbing it jumped clear as it fell, but two were carried straight to the ground.

A hard impact across the middle of Sam's back took her breath away. She crashed chest first into the battlement. The pain wasn't that intense, but she found she was having difficulty judging just how badly she'd been injured from pain level alone. The stab she'd received in her leg earlier should have incapacitated her with agony, but it had felt more like a terrifically bad cramp.

Status update: Received 8 damage to torso. Current Health 15.

The words flashed briefly in red across the upper periphery of her vision before fading away. It was almost as if they were in response to her wondering about how damaged she was. Which might well have been the case. Her movement was directed by her thoughts here. It made sense that game commands would work the same way.

Whatever the case, it seemed like that one shot had

removed about a third of her remaining health. She could still move, but she didn't want to get hit again. She whirled, bringing her shield up just in time to block a second sword blow. The shield twisted in her hand, sending most of the force of the attack off to her left side. The sword struck the battlement stones with a clang, striking sparks.

She still had her spear, and stabbed toward her opponent. He parried with his own shield. Behind him another man was climbing over the wall from the third ladder. More would be on them in moments. She had to finish this quickly.

The enemy warrior lashed out with his sword flashing. He landed a rapid series of four strikes, each one hammering hard on her defenses. Sam blocked them all with her shield, but was forced to give a few footsteps. He was backing her up, giving the enemy even more room to get onto the wall. Her shield arm was tiring. His weapon arm had to be growing weaker as well. But the grin on his face said he was confident of winning, and he strode forward at her with another attack.

Sam thrust out low with her spear. He parried the blow down easily, but she hadn't really been aiming for his leg. She'd been trying to get her spear between his legs — and the spearhead skittered off stones precisely where she'd hoped it would. She took one more blow on her shield as she ducked in close to him, swinging the butt end of the spear upward.

The shaft of the spear tangled in his legs. Sam saw his eyes widen as he realized what she'd done, a bare moment before he lost his balance. Her shield bashed into his chest as the spear twisted between his legs. He tumbled forward from the rampart, falling headfirst into the courtyard inside the walls.

"You wanted to get in," she panted. "Be my guest."

"Die, Blue!"

Sam raised her shield to block the spear strike from the next man. Her arm was so tired that she barely stopped the attack in time. There were two warriors facing her. Apparently she warranted the full attention of the fresh attackers coming over the wall, she thought wryly. She shifted into a defensive stance as both spears lashed out in tandem. She blocked one, but the second traced a fiery line across her already wounded leg. She backed away, giving them more room. Another man was climbing over the rampart behind the spearmen. She watched an arrow take him in the chest, and he spun backward onto the ground.

More spear blows rained down on her. She gave ground, barely attacking at all now. Sam put everything she could put into keeping those deadly flashing points away from her. Then her back thumped against the door. She was out of room. A spear banged hard against her shield, splintering the wood. A few more blows and the thing would shatter entirely.

But like magic, a spearhead sprouted from the chest of the man in front of her. He gaped down at the wound before collapsing to his knees and then crumpling face-first into the stonework. The man beside him had time to try to turn before a now-familiar axe cleaved his skull.

"Good job distracting those louts," Harald said. He was flanked by two more men wearing blue bands. "We've cleared this wall. You up for coming with us to finish this battle?"

She was exhausted beyond measure, but Sam nodded grimly. She'd come this far. She wasn't going to stop now. Harald jogged off, barking orders as he went. Men from the wall shoved off the last of the ladders and then fell behind him in ranks as they made their way down a flight of stairs into the courtyard. Sam gritted her teeth, took a firm grip on her spear and what was left of her shield, and followed.

5

Samantha had some of her wind back by the time she had reached the courtyard and caught up with Harald's force. She thought about checking her status, and the display popped up on her vision again for a moment.

Health 11/30, Stamina 33/100, Mana 0/0.

Judging by the numbers, she wasn't in that great shape. She'd toughed it out through some rough times in the past though. It wasn't like she could just back down now. Or could she? This was just a game, after all. It wasn't like real lives were at stake. She'd fought because there was an immediate threat, before. After Harald saved her, she'd stood beside him because he'd helped her out. It made sense to repay the favor.

But the immediate danger was past. Men — and women, she noticed — patrolled all four walls now. The attack was over, at least for the time being. Whatever counterstrike Harald was organizing didn't have anything to do with her.

Sam had never backed down from a challenge in her life, though. Whether this place was real or not, it felt real.

Deep down where it counted, the place felt as solid as her regular life. She took her place in the back rank of Harald's war party. There were about twenty warriors with him in all. Mostly men, but a few unsmiling women stood there as well. Each fighter looked grim and ready to launch themselves into action.

"Open the gate!" Harald called.

"Leave it closed," a second voice called from somewhere behind them. Sam turned to see a young, yellow haired warrior standing on the rampart near the back of the fort, where it met the inner keep. She had no idea who he was, but judging by the gilded armor he wore and the consternation his order caused in the ranks around her, he must be someone important.

"Earl Thorsten. We have them on the run," Harald called out to him. "We move on them now, we can crush them for the rest of the day."

"Or we can stand fast and defend my keep," Thorsten replied. "You all leave and die in some ambush, then their warriors return and who holds this place?"

"I'll not be hemmed in here when the fight is out there," Harald replied.

There were a few murmurs of assent from the warriors around Sam. But others looked less certain, like they were unsure which person to follow. She had no qualms, though. She didn't know who this Thorsten was, but she hadn't seen him on the walls during the fight. Harald had helped her. The least she could do would be to repay the favor. While the two men argued, she slipped up the stairs beside the gates, taking the steps two at a time in her haste to reach the top.

With all the attention on the arguing warlords, she was able to slip into the gatehouse without being noticed. One man was on duty there. His hands were on a big wheel which Sam assumed controlled the gate. But his face wore a deep frown. His sword was sheathed at his side, his shield resting up against a wall of the gatehouse.

Sam tapped him on the shoulder with her spear. He turned, startled, and reached for his blade. She held the spear tip steady near his throat and shook her head.

"I think you ought to just open the gate, friend," Sam said.

"Woman, Thorsten will make us both pay for this. I beg you, leave off," he replied.

"I don't think so," she said. "Open it. Now."

Still shaking his head, the man did as she bid. He started spinning the wheel, and there was a groaning noise below as the massive gates shuddered open. Sam tipped her head in a thank you, and dashed back out the door again.

"Any of you who leave, don't you dare come back to this place!" Thorsten was roaring. Harald had already slipped out, and it seemed like at least half his force was following him. Others had elected to stay behind. As Sam sprinted down the steps to rejoin Harald, Thorsten spotted her.

"You on the stairs!" he called out. Sam froze for a moment and looked across at him. "I've marked you. You directly defied my orders, woman. You'll pay for that."

"Maybe so," Sam shouted back. "But not today!"

"Close the damned gates!" Thorsten said. "I want her caught!"

Sam had the distinct impression she did not want to be caught. She sprinted forward for all she was worth. Luckily the men in the courtyard had all been planning to go with Harald before Thorsten ordered them to stay. Two of them tried to converge on her, but one of the other men dropped his spear to the ground. It slid out directly in front of the two men chasing Sam, and both of them tripped, falling to their knees.

The spearman tilted his head to the side, nodding toward the gate with a grin. The message was clear — get out while she could!

The gates were already rumbling shut. She dashed toward them and slipped through the gap with only seconds to spare before the thing slammed shut once more.

Harald waited just outside. He clapped her on the back. "Well done. Knew I saw something in you up there. Glad you've decided to come along."

"Not sure I had much choice. That guy was kinda pissed."

"Oh, Thorsten? He's a piece of work," Harald said. "Yes, you're better off with us. Come on then. We want to move out before he gets the idea of ordering men to put arrows into us."

The area around the fort was only open for a hundred or so meters. Past that lay a dark wood. It was toward the forest that Harald starting moving, taking up a light jog that reminded Sam of an airborne shuffle. It was the sort of run that you could keep up all day if you had to. She realized that she was still barefoot. That was something she'd need to remedy as soon as possible, but although her feet were a little sore the ground didn't seem to injure them the way it would have in the real world. One plus for the reduced pain scale of the virtual world, perhaps.

They entered the forest, and immediately the day felt more gloomy. The trees here were taller than any Sam had ever seen. They towered scores of feet above the ground, and were wide enough about that two people would have a hard time wrapping their arms around them. Ferns and other small scrub grew here and there on the forest floor, but there were also patches where the canopy overhead was simply too dense for anything to grow below the trees.

"They went this way," Harald said. He pointed off toward the west.

"How can you tell?" Sam asked.

"Broken ferns. Scuffed dirt. I have a good Tracking skill," Harald said.

"You seem to have all sorts of skills," she said.

"I've been here for a long time, girl."

Including Harald and Sam, their war band numbered fourteen in all. She wondered how many people they were chasing, and what sort of fight they were going to face when they found them. After an hour or so walking, Harald ordered everyone to stop, and held a finger to his lips for silence. He darted ahead, quickly blending into the shadows of the forest ahead.

A few minutes later he returned. He beckoned all to gather close around him before whispering to them.

"I've located what's left of the force. They're resting ahead. They had two lookouts," he said.

"Had?" one warrior asked.

"Had," Harald confirmed with a grin. "There are still twenty warriors in their band, though. It looks to me like they are waiting for reinforcements. If they get more troops, they could have enough to overrun Thorsten's fort, or one of the others along the border."

"We'll be outnumbered," one of the men pointed out. "We could just return to the fort and warn Thorsten."

"We'll have surprise on our side if their lookouts are dead," Sam said. "Besides, Thorsten didn't seem like the forgive and forget type."

There were a few chuckles and nods at that.

"Agreed then?" Harald asked. "We hit them hard, take

their heads and their loot, and then we march to Blendrake Faste. Let Thorsten fend for himself and sweat it out a little."

The course agreed upon, Harald set to going over a plan of battle. Sam felt herself growing excited despite herself. This was going to be fun.

6

Sam crept through the woods, following Harald. Behind her trailed a man and woman, two of the other warriors who'd followed Harald from the keep. The pair had stayed close together throughout the journey. Little bits of their body language, like a small touch or a silent smile to the other partner made Sam think they were likely a couple. She wondered if they were together in the real world as well, or if this relationship only existed virtually.

The thought brought her back to wondering how the hell she was going to get out of this game. Sam fully admitted that she was having a lot more fun than she'd ever expected. She could see the appeal of this sort of virtual reality, even if she preferred the real to the surreal.

But she pictured Jeff sitting there, watching her play, and her temper boiled at the idea. After this fight was over, she resolved to ask Harald how she could log off. Surely, someone who knew as much about the game as he did would be able to help.

"When we get close, unleash Hel," Harald whispered.

He kept his voice barely audible. They must be very close to their enemy. "Geri and Alwyn — use your bows. Sam and I will keep them off you."

Sam swallowed hard. The bows the couple carried ought to do a lot of damage, but she hoped they were good enough with them. If twenty screaming warriors rushed them, she and Harald were going to last about ten seconds.

The archers remained a little behind them as they continued their advance. Sam heard voices ahead. Their rumblings were still too distant to make out individual words, but they were not far ahead. She rounded a tree and saw a guard leaning against another tree not far ahead. She darted back, hoping that she hadn't been seen. Peeking around the corner again, she realized that the guard wasn't moving. Not even a little bit. Further inspection showed that he had blood leaking down from his neck, where a big gash had opened his veins.

Harald had been thorough. To anyone back in the camp, it looked like the guard was still standing there at his post.

She continued forward, creeping softly to stand beside the dead man. Sam avoided the blood pooled around his feet, shivering a little. In some ways this game was entirely too real.

They must have gotten close enough to the camp. Sam heard an arrow whistle past her tree, and then a cry of pain as it struck home. Another yell sounded as a second arrow struck its mark. There was a hue and cry, everyone rising at once and looking about them for the attackers. Two more arrows slammed home before they realized where the shots were coming from, but once they did the warriors set up a wall of shields to defend themselves.

Two of them were down. Two more were wounded but still held the line with the rest. Eighteen warriors formed their line in all, and as a unit they marched forward from the clearing where they'd been resting into the woods. Two more arrows darted in, but they slammed into shields instead of bodies. That wall of shields wasn't letting much through.

"Just a couple of archers," one of the men shouted.

"Watch for others. Stay close!" another replied.

"Rush them!" shouted a third.

The latter man followed his own advice as he yelled, leaving the line. He still had his shield up guarding his head and upper body. Four of his fellows followed close behind him, doing the same. With their heads ducked down behind shields, they couldn't see where they were going very well.

Sam stuck her spear out along the ground as the first passed by her hiding place. He tripped and fell face-first into the ground. Not a moment after he landed, two arrows sprouted from his back. He didn't move again.

With a yell Harald came out from behind his own tree and smashed another of the men in the face with his axe. He fell with a yell. Harald swung at another of the warriors, but he blocked the blow with his shield. The blow distracted him enough that Sam was able to stick the point of her spear into the back of his leg. The wounded limb buckled, dropping him to the ground. Harald's axe descended a moment later.

The remaining two men retreated back to their line. Sam yelled after the retreating warriors. She raised her shield and spear, ready to advance after them, but Harald grabbed her arm.

"Now we pull back," he said. "Too many there."

"I'm with you," she replied.

They began picking their path away from the enemy line. Seeing them retreating, the shield wall advanced again.

If anything they were moving even more rapidly this time. The trap had been sprung, after all. There were only four fighters against their fifteen.

The archers fired one more ineffective volley against the shield wall and then began their own retreat. Sam was just about ready to bolt for the woods. The shield wall was coming on at a light jog now. Any moment and they would turn that into a full sprint.

"Wait," Harald said, seeing her tense. "Almost time."

Then she heard shouts from back in the clearing where the green troops had been gathered. Their formation halted, the men peering back behind them. Another shield wall had formed, and the greens weren't sure at first if they were friends or foes.

The answer came with a pair of short, thrown spears which took down two of the green warriors. With a massive battle cry the other ten warriors of Harald's band rushed forward at the greens' line.

They turned to face this new threat, only to be peppered by more arrows from behind. When two of the green warriors tried to get to the archers, they ran into Sam and Harald instead. Harald made short work of his opponent and then rushed in at the back of the enemy line.

Sam found herself face to face with another woman fighter. She had an axe in one hand and shield in the other. Darting in close, the woman hammered in a blow at Sam, which she took on the shield. The vibration thrummed through her hand and forearm. Bits of wood flew from her shield where the axe had damaged it.

Another blow, and a third, and Sam's shield was coming apart. The top board broke away entirely. It wasn't going to take many more strikes to shatter the thing entirely. Her own blows hadn't been very effective at all. Her spear didn't seem to be able to get through the woman's own shield defense, and it wasn't doing much damage to the shield itself either.

It was time to try something different. Sam rushed in, bashing the woman with what was left of her shield. Wood splintered and cracked under the impact as her shield broke apart completely. But the blow was strong enough to knock the woman over backward. She tumbled to the forest floor.

Target stunned! Damage inflicted: 5

Sam stabbed downward, taking her under her ribs with the spear. The green woman's eyes widened and she clenched her fingers around the spear shaft, but the wound was already mortal. She made a gurgling sound, and died.

Panting for breath, Sam leaned into her spear for a moment. The battle up ahead was already coming to a close. Her side had won handily. The two-pronged attack plus the element of surprise had been more than enough to overwhelm the larger enemy force. She looked down at the body on the ground in front of her.

She'd trained to kill for years. That's what one did, in the military. But she'd never actually killed a person before. Sam wondered if this experience really counted or not. It felt real. She could smell the blood and for the rest of her life she'd remember the way the woman's eyes widened with shock as she died. Feeling or seeming real wasn't the same thing as being real, though.

As fun a diversion as this place had turned out to be, it wasn't real. Real people don't respawn and come back to fight again. Real battles were over things that mattered, not pixel loot and bytes of data. It was time to get back to her world, where the things she did mattered.

7

Harald's force had taken only two casualties in the battle. The opposing force was wrecked. Between the arrows and the attack from two sides, not a single green fighter had survived. As Sam watched, the blue warriors went through the bodies, picking them over for valuables. They stripped away bits of armor, weapons, and even a few pouches that had coins or some other valuables inside. Sam walked over to Harald, who was pulling loot from a body just like the others. She hoped to get a few questions answered.

"Here, take these," he said as she walked up. She caught the pair of leather boots he threw her way. "They look about the right size."

She slipped them on. They were a little snug, but they ought to fit after a little wear... Leather would stretch out after she'd put a few miles into them. But no — she wasn't going to be putting miles into anything here. She was done. It was time to go home. She made a firm line of her mouth, setting her thoughts again to the task. Why was it so hard to think of leaving?

"Harald, how does this work?" she asked, waving her hand at the bodies they were looting.

"Valhalla is full drop, except for a few special items," Harald said. He patted his axe. "My weapon here, for example, is bound. It won't drop even if I die. Things like that are rare and exceptionally valuable though. Most of the time you lose everything if you're killed. You'll come back looking — well, like you did when you arrived today."

"So all of this stuff...?" she asked.

"We'll carry it back with us. Some of it folks will save away for a rainy day when they die and don't have anything handy. You can drop some stuff in your Vault. The rest will get sold. With coin you can buy better gear."

"Makes sense," she said. Sam had heard Jeff rattle on about his games enough that she had a general understanding of how this stuff worked. But she was letting herself get side-tracked again. "Listen, Harald. This has been fun. But I need to get home again. How do I log out?"

He blinked, staring at her strangely for a moment. Then, rather than answering her question he reached down toward the body again, pulling up a new shield and a short sword. "You'll want these. The spear is a nice weapon, but something for close combat is a good idea, and your shield was broken."

Sam didn't take the items he held out. Part of her wanted to. It was like a seductive voice whispered in her ear that she should take them, arm herself, make herself stronger... She shook away those thoughts again, fighting to keep her mind focused on her goal.

"I mean it. I didn't choose to log in here. How do I get out of the game?" she asked. "Is there a button? A command?"

"You're serious," he said. He chewed his lower lip,

rubbing his chin in thought. "You really have no idea where you are? Or how you got here?"

Sam shook her head. "Last thing I remember, I was on the job, working on a case. Then I woke up here. I don't know what happened in the middle...the memories are fuzzy."

"That's normal," he said. "The upload process can't manage short term memory as well as long term memory. You tend to lose a little recent information. Samantha, you'd better sit down for this."

He gestured to a log. Uncertain what this was about but wanting the information Harald clearly had, Sam sat. He stalked in front of her, looking uncomfortable.

"It's Valhalla Online," he said at last. He turned sideways to look at her, but Sam's confusion must have continued to show on her face. "It was a big deal in the media. You never heard about it?"

She shook her head. "I was in West Point the last four years. Kinda busy."

"Shit. You're a kid," he muttered.

She was not, and was about to protest him calling her that, but he waved her down. "To me, you're a kid. To most of us. The people living here in this world, most of us are over sixty. Some folks here are eighty. I've met one woman who was a hundred years old. You're what, twenty?"

"Twenty four," she replied.

"Right. A kid." Harald sighed. "OK. About ten years ago, they first began experimenting with ways to upload consciousness to computers. You heard about that?"

Sam nodded. She'd caught bits of that in the news. It seemed like tech that was going to continue to evolve over time. Back in the 'Point, people joked around about the Army uploading minds directly to tanks or artillery pieces, so that you wouldn't have crew anymore. You'd literally be a part of your machine. Or a copy of your mind would be, anyway — the real you would be out there in the world doing the same old things, while the uploaded copy of your identity would run a war machine. The concept was both interesting and creepy at the same time.

"Well, four years ago — probably about the same time you started college — someone developed the tech to take brain-scans at the moment of death, or as close to death as possible, and upload them to a computer. Immortality via silicon, you get it?" Harald said. "But because uploaded personalities don't have rights, aren't seen as living things with rights, they couldn't just be allowed to roam free. So the company made this game, Valhalla Online."

"People pay big bucks to have their consciousness uploaded to the game. An afterlife, for those terrified there wouldn't be an afterlife," Harald said. He waved his hand around. "Everything you see around you, this entire virtual world? It's all a construct to keep busy the memories and personae that we had uploaded as we died."

Sam blinked. That didn't sound anything like the game Jeff had described. But come to think of it, she had heard something about that on the news, hadn't she? Fundamentalist Christians protesting, or something like that? God's will being overturned by an artificial afterlife? But how had she gotten into this place? It wasn't like she was...

Sam froze, not wanting to finish that thought.

"Yeah, I can see you get it now," Harald said. "Everyone in this game is dead. We are the lingering memories of people who died, anyway. There isn't any logging off, because none of us have a body to return to. Not anymore."

8

Sam was glad she was already sitting. The way her hands and legs began to shake, she was certain she would have fallen down if she'd still been standing up. She was breathing too fast and she knew it, but she couldn't get her breath back under control.

"That's not possible," she said. "I'm not dead. I'd remember...something! Right?"

Harald shook his head sadly. "Not always. Like I said, the short term memory is often a little fragmented. It doesn't always survive the transition."

Sam closed her eyes and took a deep breath. Every lungful felt real, but she knew that was illusion. This was just pixels. The sensations were artificial. But were they artificial stimuli being fed into her brain? Or into a complex set of algorithms mimicking her sense of self? How could one even know?

"Wouldn't I need to volunteer for this?" she asked. "I didn't even know about Valhalla Online. How could I sign up for this without even knowing about it?"

"That is unusual," Harald said. "I've been here since just

about the beginning. There used to be a hefty fee involved. I paid seven figures to the game to ensure I would be here forever. Of course, I got a premium package. You could get in for only six figures."

"More money than I've ever had," Sam said.

"I doubt it got much cheaper. Maybe your family...? After you're dead, consent stops being such a big issue," Harald said. "It's possible that someone could have done something post-mortem if they got to you in time."

Sam thought about that. Her mother might be nuts enough to try to do something like this, just to keep her 'baby girl' alive at least in spirit a little longer. She couldn't imagine her father ever allowing it, though. None of this made sense.

Of course, she'd signed all sorts of waivers on joining the Army, and she hadn't bothered reading most of them. But she couldn't picture the military paying a ton of money to stick her brain in here. How would they benefit? There was a more likely answer.

"This is just a virtual world, right?" she asked, opening her eyes.

Harald nodded. "Yes. More or less."

"So I could just be hooked up to it with a virtual gaming suit, right?" Sam asked. "Just like in a regular game?"

It was the only idea that made sense. Someone had drugged her and hooked her up to this game. Somehow she was still alive out there, somewhere, and connected to the system. It still begged the question of who had done this. But if she could find a way to get a message out, then maybe she could let people know where she was. They could find her and rescue her.

"It's a closed system," Harald said. "It's supposed to be damned near unhackable. There's no way to get an external mind in except through the company machines and those are supposed to just upload the mind. If they did that to a living body..." His voice trailed off.

"What would happen?" Sam asked.

"I don't know," Harald said. "In all my years here, I've never heard of a case like yours. I've never heard of anyone here who hadn't paid big money to get in."

Sam's hands were shaking a bit less. She worked to control her emotions, to quell the roiling anxiety that threatened to overwhelm her. She could not possibly be dead. She was not going to accept that. There had to be a way to fight it. All she needed to do was figure out how.

"There's no way to log off then, because the game was never designed for players who had anything to log off to, right?" she asked.

"Correct."

"What about messages?" she asked. "Is there a way I can reach anyone outside?"

It made sense. Immortality was only cool if you had some way to reach the outside world, right? People would want to talk with loved ones. Family would want to be able to pass messages back and forth. If she could reach people out there, then they could get her out of here.

Or at least tell her what the hell had happened.

"There is. But the way is hard. Most people don't manage it," Harald said. "Those who do tend to tire of it quickly and move on."

"I've never backed down from a challenge," Sam said, rising back to her feet. "How do I do it?"

"Easier to show you than tell you," Harald said. "It'll be dark soon. Come with me to Blendrake Faste. I'll show you there."

Sam managed to acquire a set of linen pants and a belt,

along with the boots, axe, and new shield. All together it was a nice little setup, although she still missed her pistol. She put on the new clothing and slid the axe into a loop on her belt.

Once every member of the group had taken any items which were immediately useful to them, the rest was bundled up and divided up for transport. They still had over an hour to walk to reach the fort, Sam was told. Although it was unlikely that they would be attacked this late in the day, it was still possible. Scouts out to either side and their front warded the band as they made their way through the forest.

The others were all-too willing to help the 'newbie' find her way in the world. Harald suggested she not pass along word of her 'special circumstances' to the others, as it would only make them uncomfortable. Sam agreed to keep quiet about it, at least for the moment. The last thing she needed was to have everyone around her think she was nuts.

Alwyn, one of the archers, walked alongside her and helped her learn to navigate the basic menus available to all players. Almost immediately, Sam saw a new prompt appear.

Your Shield skill is now Level 2!

Alwyn showed her how to call up her Statistics screen. This was an overlay on her vision, like the others, but it was much more detailed. A wealth of information flooded across her sight. It was too much to take it all in for now, so she closed it down.

"It looks like I have a lot to learn," Sam said. How much of this was she going to need to know to get her message out? She had no idea. Just Harald's assurances that it was possible.

"You don't need to do it all on your first day," Alwyn said, laughing and clapping Sam across the back. "You have forever here in Valhalla."

"Who were you, out there?" Sam asked. She didn't want to talk about forever. Not right then, anyway. "Before you came here, I mean."

The laugh died, and Alwyn's smile faded in an instant. "I don't like to think about those times much. About what was. I prefer to focus on the life that is. My life today is much better than what I once had."

"I'm sorry. I didn't mean to bring up bad memories," Sam said.

"No, you didn't know," Alwyn replied. "But you'll find that most of us prefer to look forward, rather than back."

Was that because life was so bad for them all out there in the real world, and so much better here? Or was it because thinking about the outside world made them recall that their life here was a lie? That they were literally ghosts in a machine, the memories of people who had been alive? Sam kept those questions to herself, but she couldn't help wondering them. She held fast to the idea that she was not one of these people. That somewhere out there in the real world was her living body, waiting for her to exit the game and wake up.

Would she want to go on as one of these people, if that were not the case? This game was fun, but it wasn't real. It was make believe. To live forever but never have any real impact on the world seemed like a nightmare to Sam.

All at once the forest thinned around them, and then broke into a massive clearing. As they left the trees, Sam looked ahead and saw a small hill, with a fort atop it much like the one she'd awoken in earlier. In fact, this keep looked almost identical to that one, right down to the blue banners draped from the walls. Harald was shouting to someone up on the walls, and in response to his call the gates rumbled open.

"We've made it, friends!" Harald shouted. "Blendrake Faste! Mead and good food await us all inside!"

With any luck some answers awaited as well. Sam would give up all the mead and food in the world for just a handful of those.

9

Cheers greeted them as they came in through the gates. Warriors lined the walls and hollered down at Harald. He shouted back in good humor. Sam could tell he was both well known and highly regarded here. The tone of their welcome was very different from the belligerent manner with which Thorsten had treated him back at the other keep.

Off to one side of the courtyard were a series of shops, built into the lee of the wall. Harald headed straight toward one, the rest of the band trailing in his wake.

"What have you brought me this time?" sighed a scruffy bald man behind the counter. "More trash?"

"Mostly, yes, but a few nice bits," Harald said. Then to Sam and the other bearing their bundles, he said, "Lay it out for Olaf. He'll need to paw over it all to give us a price."

"I don't paw, you goat," Olaf said. "I examine with my gimlet eye."

They laid their bundles down on the store's big countertop one after another. Olaf opened each bundle in turn and perused the items. Most of them he dumped into a big bin behind him. A few he set off to the side. Sam didn't understand the system he was using to divide items up, but it was clearly one he'd practiced for a long time.

Olaf would lift an item up to examine it, turning it over a few times in front of his face. He might tug at it a bit or test the edge on a weapon. Then he either tossed the item into the bin or much more carefully set it down once more on the counter.

Sam grew bored watching him work and wandered a few feet away. She'd left the other keep this morning in such a rush she hadn't even gotten the name of the place, let alone been able to look around. There were four shops in a row here. One was a stable, with a few horses inside. Then Olaf's little shop of random goods. Next in the row there was a smaller shop with a closed door. Sam couldn't tell precisely what was there, but the sign above the door had a shield and crossed axes on it, and read 'Rewards of the Realm'.

The last shop caught her eye. It had a series of runic symbols drawn not only on the sign, but also along the mantle of the doorway to enter. The sign above the door called the place 'Mystic Mail'.

She drifted over in that direction, curious. Was this the means of communication that Harald planned to show her? Curious, she stepped up to the door, which lay slightly ajar, and knocked quietly.

"Enter," called a female voice from inside.

Sam opened the door and stepped in. The space inside was small, perhaps ten by ten feet. Long lengths of string with rattling beads dangled from the ceiling to drape across the walls. Sam touched some as she entered, and shuddered when she realized the beads were bits of bone. They were too small for her to be certain what sort of animal they'd come from, but they looked like they could have been human finger bones.

A single figure was seated on a small chair across the room from her. In front of the chair was a square table, sitting only a few feet above the ground. The figure was wearing a hooded robe, but Sam could have sworn she recognized the voice from somewhere.

"Please sit," the woman said. She gestured to a chair opposite her own. Sam crossed the short distance and sat down.

From the new angle, she could better see the strange woman's face, and realized immediately why the voice had been so familiar.

"You!" Sam said.

It was Helga. Or close enough to be her twin, anyway. Sam realized the hair was the wrong color. This woman had jet black her streaked with white. But her face was the same as the woman who'd given Sam her spear this morning.

"I am Frenrula, mystic seer of this keep," the woman said. "I do not believe we have met, but I am one Guide of many in this world, so you might have seen one of my sisters. How can I help you?"

"I'm not sure. Can you help me send a message?" Sam asked. This must be a computer controlled being, like the Guide she had met when she first woke up. Olaf had seemed real enough, but she hadn't questioned him enough to know for sure. Were all of the shops run by the computer? Or were some of them controlled by real people?

"Of course! To whom would you like to send mail?" Frenrula replied.

"To my parents," Sam said. She held her breath, hoping that this would work.

"I'm sorry," Frenrula replied, with a tone which did seem

to register deep sadness. "You cannot send messages out of Valhalla at your current level. Only those most favored of the Gods can reach out into Midgard and speak with those still living there."

Sam wanted to scream. It was clearly possible to get a message out. But this damned machine wasn't going to let her do it? She gritted her teeth together. Yelling at a computer wasn't going to help make her situation any better. "How does one become favored of the Gods?"

"You must pass through all of the Realms and reach Asgard itself. There, in the final mead hall of true Valhalla, where only the most puissant of warriors stay by Odin and Freya's sides, you can beseech of them the boon of reaching out to Midgard."

"Midgard being Earth, and the people outside of this game," Sam said.

"Just so."

Sam sighed. There had to be another way of doing this. The Guide was making it sound like she needed to basically beat the game just to get an email sent. That couldn't be right. "Is there any other way I can communicate with my family?" she asked.

"No, child. The dead must remain divided from the living except in the most extreme of cases," Frenrula said. "Imagine if the dead were able to speak to the living on a whim. There would be no rest for those still on Midgard. There would be no way for those left behind to set aside grief and move on with their own lives."

"But I'm not dead!" Sam said, frustrated into almost yelling. The concept made sense. The avatars in this game were all dead people, the uploaded memories and personalities of the dead, anyway. If her grandparents were constantly sending her texts from beyond the grave it would drive her nuts. Were they really dead? Or just mostly dead? The questions would drive people mad, and the pain of wondering would be too much to bear for many.

But her scenario was different. All she wanted was to get a message out so that she could find out how she'd gotten into this game in the first place. She hadn't signed up. She hadn't paid the huge fees Harald spoke of. Sam wanted to think that her body was still alive out there, hooked up to a machine that had put her into this world. Worst case, even if she was dead she wanted to know it. To end the wondering. To have some finality for herself, and find out who the hell had done this to her.

"I'm sorry, child," Frenrula said. She reached out and gently patted Sam's hand. "But if you are in Valhalla, then you have assuredly passed from the mortal worlds into the life beyond. Your life on Midgard is over. Only through the gifts of the gods can you reach out into that world again."

10

Harald came over to see Sam as she walked slowly from the Mystic Mail shop. He hesitated a moment and then seemed to make a decision before walking to her side. Sam wasn't entirely sure she wanted the company just then. Part of her would rather be alone with her thoughts. But she didn't chase him away, either.

"Didn't hear what you were hoping, eh?" Harald asked.

"No," Sam said. "Was that where you were taking me?"

Harald nodded. "One place, anyway. But I already knew what she was going to tell you. You just weren't going to hear it from me."

Sam wanted to protest that, but he wasn't wrong. She'd already denied what he was trying to tell her more than once. This wasn't a problem she could solve with a quick email out to the authorities. The entire game was set up to prevent contact between those inside and those outside.

It all made sense, in a way. The living had rights which needed to be protected. The uploaded avatars of the dead did not, at least not the same sort of rights their living relatives did.

Sam thought it might be cruel to those inside as well. Imagine if they could reach out to those they loved by mail, but never see them. They could never be there again, never touch, or hold, or kiss those left behind. With contact cut off the avatars of the dead could build new lives for themselves instead of pining for what they had lost. Blocking contact from inside to out protected both parties.

That didn't mean she was about to give up though. Her case was unique. She had no evidence that she was actually dead, and quite a lot that she wasn't. She'd never signed a consent to be uploaded to Valhalla. She'd never paid. Either someone had gone to a lot of trouble to illegally store her here after her death — for reasons Sam couldn't even begin to fathom — or her body was still out there somewhere, breathing and hooked into the game.

"Maybe I wouldn't have listened to you," Sam agreed. "I'm still not completely convinced that you're right. But it sounds like this is going to be harder than I thought."

"You think you have what it takes to go all the way to Odin's hall, girl?" Harald asked. He chuckled and shook his head. "Most newbies do. Some of them even make it as far as the third realm before giving it up. It's the rare man who makes it past that point."

"Good thing I'm not a man, then," Sam snapped back. She was a trained soldier surrounded by the dead remnants of a bunch of old, rich people. How hard could it be to beat this game, after all?

Harald laughed even harder. "You have me there. But seriously, Sam. This is no easy task you're undertaking."

"You've said that. But you're not telling me what's so hard about beating a stupid game," she said.

"It's not..." He paused. Sam could tell from the way his cheeks pinked that she'd struck a nerve. Didn't want his video game being called what it was, did he?

Harald sucked in a breath and continued. "It's not a game for us. This is our home. This is our reality. For better or worse, this is all we have. All any of us will ever have again. You demean the life we all have here by calling it that. This is our life you're belittling."

She'd hurt him, and that hadn't been her intent. Sam realized she was frightened and hurting herself. The pain of not knowing if she was dead or alive was eating away at her. It wasn't going to do her any good to annoy one of the few allies she had here, though.

"I'm sorry," she said. "I wasn't thinking of it that way. I should have shown more respect."

"You'll need to, if you plan to win through. Nothing less than complete commitment will do where you want to go." Harald held out a small pouch. It jingled as he tossed it to her. "Your share of the coins from the loot."

She caught it and realized she didn't have any pockets to tuck the thing into. Another annoyance about this world. They seemed to keep coming, one after another. Sam was about to tie it to her belt when she saw Harald shaking his head.

"Not there," he said. "A cutpurse will have it from you in a half a breath. Tuck it into your shirt. Maybe tie it to your... you know." he made motions around his chest to mirror where her bra was. She laced the strings onto the loop of leather between her breasts, and hung the purse inside the leather vest she wore. He was right. It ought to be more secure in there.

"Now what?" she asked.

"Now you come with me, and see what you're trying to let yourself in for," he replied.

They left the courtyard for the main hall, which occupied the entire bottom floor of the inner keep. Huge tables filled most of the room, heaping with food and flagons of drink. Dozens of men and women crowded at the tables. Most of them were eating and drinking, speaking to one another in boastfully loud voices all the while. Sam spotted a pair arm-wrestling at one table. A few warriors nursed quiet mugs of ale by themselves, set off from those carousing the evening away. But most of the tables were full of boisterous, loud, and openly smiling people.

Almost all of them were young. In fact, Sam had only seen a few people with white hair at all. Harald was one. Olaf another. She wracked her thoughts but couldn't recall seeing another person who looked to be older than forty since she'd arrived. That made her wonder how people's appearances were decided, and what she herself looked like. It wasn't like there were mirrors all over to view herself. Her hair seemed to be about the same color. Her skin tone looked familiar to her. But Sam wondered if her face was still the one she knew from looking at her reflection above the bathroom sink every morning, or if she would see a stranger in the mirror now.

"Why is your hair white?" Sam asked, as she followed Harald past all the tables to the far end of the hall.

"When everyone else looks so young?" Harald said. "You're guessing I picked the look, and you'd be right. Sometimes it's just how I feel. Old, compared to all these young pups newly come to the world. I've seen too much, girl. Some things you just can't un-see, or un-feel."

He dropped the matter. Not wanting to irritate him again, Sam let it rest. Harald was an interesting conundrum.

He seemed respected by many, but he didn't rule one of these keeps. He didn't hesitate to openly disobey orders from the man who'd seemed in charge of the other keep, and the war band she'd fought with today had followed him. His white hair set him apart, but it was more than that. He had secrets that she was curious to know more about. Why was he bothering to help her at all, for that matter?

The far end of the hall had fewer people gathered around. Several stone steps led to a massive fireplace set against the wall. A handful stood there, staring into the flames like they were seeing something other than fire. Sam glanced at the flickering arcs of orange and yellow, and for a moment she thought she saw something else as well. Then it was gone.

"The hearth is a place of power inside each keep," Harald told her. "From here you can see what's going on in this realm, and in the realms beyond."

"How many realms are there?" she asked.

"Nine. We're in the Twilight Lands right now, a place for newer warriors to learn the ways of this world before moving on to the true Norse realms," he said.

Sam wondered why he was here then. Harald had said that he'd been in Valhalla Online almost since the beginning. Why would he still be in these Twilight Realms? It didn't speak well for her odds of winning through.

"After this place there are eight others, one for each of the Norse realms of legend, except Midgard," Harald said.

"Midgard?" she asked.

"Earth. Where humans live."

That made sense, in a way. They were dwelling in the great beyond, the life after — even if it was just a game version of it. The realm they had already left behind would be Midgard.

"But I thought this was Valhalla. Isn't that supposed to be in Asgard?" she asked.

"You know something about the Norse religion?" Harald asked. He seemed surprised.

"I watched the Thor movies," Sam said. "That's about it."

"Well, this is Valhalla Online. It's based on the old Norse myths, but they didn't write down an awful lot about their universe. Or if they did, not a lot survived. That left a lot available for the imagination. The people who built this world didn't want anyone to get bored too quickly. They set up a wide variety of worlds, each with their own unique challenges," he said. "Beat one world, and you win through to the next, and so on. You can also fall back down the tiers to a simpler realm if you want."

Sam was looking at the fire again. As she stared into the flames she began seeing numbers and letters appear in her vision. It seemed blurry, but the more she concentrated the better they came into focus.

There was her own name! It looked like it was at the bottom of a list. The very, very bottom, based on the number 'twelve' next to her name. The other names above hers had higher numbers, and the numbers seemed to climb as she went up the list. She thought of Harald's name, and the list scrolled rapidly. His name was third from the top, with 80,921 points. There was another name she recognized right below his — Thorsten, with 79,394 points.

"What the hell is this?" she whispered.

"What you're seeing are realm points," he said softly. "You can spend them to get upgrades to your equipment. With enough effort you can win bound items, which won't ever leave you even if you die."

"There are about a thousand warriors per instance of the Twilight Realms," Harald said. "At the end of each day those with the top hundred realm points may choose to step into the flames and move on to the next realm."

That was what she would have to do, she realized. To win her way out of these Twilight Realms and even begin her quest to beat the others, she needed to be in the top one hundred. She scrolled back to her own name. She was a very, very long way from the top of the list.

11

Sam rose early to the sound of fighting outside. She rolled from her bed quickly, slipping into her boots. Her armor still hung from a rack next to her bed. Around her spread the barracks where she'd bedded down for the night. Rows of bunks on either side of the room housed both men and women alike. It had been a little bit of a shock for her, but she wasn't quite ready to pay the copper coin a night for her own room in the fort. The coin she had won from the battle yesterday might have to last her a while.

A few of the beds were newly empty, the people who'd slept in them having risen already. Most of the people there continued to sleep, though. Sam wondered at that. Should she rouse them? If they were under attack, they might need every warrior on the walls.

She decided to peek outside before she sounded the alarm. Grabbing her weapons and shield, she padded down the hall toward the exit. It was just past dawn, and the sun wasn't in full blossom yet. The hazy remnant of a mist spread over the courtyard before her. But there were already people out there with weapons, battling.

It wasn't an attack, she realized. All of them wore the blue arm-bands she'd seen on her side before.

"Come join the practice!" Harald called out from the field. "Lord knows you could use it, newbie!"

"I kept up with you well enough yesterday!" Sam shot back. But she was smiling. Gibes were part of the fellowship in an army, and she recognized his tone of voice from her own time in the service. Some things didn't change just because one was in a virtual world instead of the real one.

Harald directed her to where she could grab some padding to wear, including a padded helmet. Then he showed her the sticks they used for practice combat, and she could see why the padding was important. They were practicing with wood swords and axes, and it looked to her like the combatants weren't holding back that much.

"Good to see you up. Not a slug-a-bed, I take it?" Harald said.

"I guess there's no mandatory wake-up call here?" she asked.

"Not hardly. But if you want to excel, you rise with the sun."

That made sense to Sam. She wondered at the people still in their beds. What were their goals, if not to improve here? She supposed there would always be those who just went with the flow and put in minimal effort. Even in 'Valhalla'. But that wasn't going to get her where she wanted to be. She was starting behind the curve. She'd need to work harder than most of the rest to catch up.

"Pain is reduced here, so the hits will only sting a bit, but you'll take damage," Harald said. "Watch your health level. It will drop as you are hit. We have healing herbs over there by the water urn that you can use to restore your health a bit if you start running low."

"Got it," Sam said. She selected a wooden shield and hand axe which closely resembled the iron one she'd been given the day before. Best to practice with something like what you had, she figured.

"Let's pair you with someone about your own size," Harald said. "Just to start."

"I can handle whoever you throw my way," Sam replied.

"Don't worry. I didn't say I'd make it easy. Alwyn, show the newbie the ropes?" he called.

The archer Sam had befriended the day before came over. She wasn't using a bow this time. Instead she had a shield just like Sam's, and a wooden sword.

"Don't take it easy on me," Sam said. "I can take it."

"Oh, I won't," Alwyn replied with a wicked smile.

The next hour was a series of lessons, each one punctuated with a bruising blow to some part of her body. Alwyn's sword struck like lightning, and it always seemed to be someplace her shield was not. Her axe only struck home twice on Alwyn's padded ribs or head. The damned thing kept turning in her hand as she struck, or she would overswing, miss, and leave herself open.

"Focus on your guard!" Alwyn said after she'd left herself open that way for the umpteenth time. If Sam never heard those words again, she'd be thrilled. She said as much.

"Then do it," Alwyn replied, laughing as she swatted aside Sam's shield and stabbed the chest pads above her heart.

Sam checked her stats. She was down to about half health. But the practice seemed to have done some good.

Your Axe skill is now Level 2!
Your Shield skill is now Level 3!

"How many skill levels are there?" Sam asked.

"I don't rightly know," Alwyn replied. "There are at least two hundred levels for each skill. But rumor says there are heroic levels above that, up to maybe two hundred and fifty. I've never met anyone with skills that high though."

"Shit. I have a long way to go," Sam said.

Alwyn laughed. "We all do! But first, breakfast."

They went into the main hall for the meal. Most of the late sleepers were beginning to rise and come in for the meal as well. Harald staked out a table for those who'd been up for the early practice, and Sam took a seat on one of the benches with the others. Somehow it didn't surprise her that most of the early risers were the same band Harald and she had fought alongside the day before.

She couldn't help but think she'd at least fallen in with a good crowd here. They chatted easily with one another, relaxing after the hard work-out. In the corner of her eye, Sam could see her stamina bar refilling quickly. Her health status was recovering as well, but much more slowly. She'd probably need more of those healing herbs after breakfast.

"Before I forget," Harald said. "Sam, you'll want to bind here at this keep. Don't want you to die in a fight later and come back at Thorsten's home base."

"Lord no," Alwyn said. "After you bearded him in his den like that, he's going to be gunning for you."

"Can he do anything? I mean, I can tell people from the same faction can hurt each other," she said, wincing as she rubbed a new bruise. Alwyn laughed and a few others around the table chuckled. "But even if he killed me, I'd just come back, right?"

"Sure. You come back at dawn the next day, if you die. But if you were bound at his keep, all he'd have to do is have someone standing there to kill you each morning as you rose," Harald said.

Sam shivered at the thought. An eternity of death after death, with no interlude between? That sounded like hell.

"Things like that don't happen often. We all tend to squash the few assholes who think it's a good idea," Harald said. "But let's not give him the chance, eh?"

"No. Let's not. How do I bind?" Sam asked.

"Walk up to the fire you saw last night. Stare into it and say the words 'I bind my spirit here'. That will make this keep your respawn point," Harald said. "There are other places you can bind. Any keep we control works. The faction castle is a safer place, but it's also usually far from the fighting. The castle can't be taken by another faction, and it's where we all respawn if the keep we're bound to gets taken and we die."

"There are other places as well," Alwyn said. "Certain dungeons or quest areas have bind-points in their beginning. Some of them will even force-bind you if you so much as enter the place!"

"Risky to bind to those though," another man added. "If you die and can't easily recover your gear, you'll be stuck with a long walk through the wilderness to get back to a friendly keep."

Sam's head whirled with the sudden influx of information. The game had a lot more nuance than she'd considered, and this was only the first world? What were the others like? It seemed like an entire new set of rules and laws to live by, and screwing up could result in awful consequences.

"How the hell am I supposed to learn all of this?" she complained.

"You never played any online RPG games...before?" Alwyn asked.

Sam shook her head.

"Most of us had. It's pretty easy to adapt to if you already know the basics from games you once played," Alwyn said.

"Except this isn't a game," one of the other men added. He raised his mug. "To our lives! May we give them meaning each day!"

The others all raised their mugs and joined the toast. Sam stared at them incredulously for a moment, but raised her own glass to join them. When in Rome, right? The utter folly of dead people toasting their lives as bytes of data in a computer game seemed lost on them. If they couldn't see it themselves, it wasn't up to her to announce the futility of their lives to them.

12

After breakfast was done Sam bound to the fire. It was as simple a process as Harald had said. She simply whispered the words under her breath. A boxy display appeared in the middle of her vision, asking her if she really wanted to switch her bind point.

Sam stared at the Yes answer, which highlighted and then activated after she held her gaze on it another moment. 'Clicking' was as simple as staring at an icon for the designated amount of time. Intent and sensors designed to detect eye contact — or simulated eye contact — handled the rest from there.

The idea of dying was still alien to her. Her whole life, it had been something to fear, a thing to be avoided. But listening to the others talk, most of them had died many times. Harald wouldn't answer when she asked him how many times he'd been returned to the grindstone. Sam had the feeling he wasn't counting anymore.

"I need to move on to reach the level where I can get a message out," Sam said to him after she was done binding. "To do that, I need to earn Realm Points, right?"

"That's right," he drawled.

"How do I do that?"

"Follow me," he said, grinning ear to ear.

She sighed and followed. What else was she going to do? She'd clearly already picked up a few RP. The fire display had told her she had twelve of them last night. Her best guess was that they came from fighting other faction members. Probably from beating them, or at least from injuring them.

"It's five points for each enemy you kill. One point for an assist," Harald said. "Capturing a keep is a thousand. Holding the keep is a thousand each day. Which is a hell of a lot harder than it sounds. Sometimes these places change hands three or four times in a single day."

"Got it," Sam replied. Her twelve points must have been two kills and two assists. She wasn't sure precisely how the game was calculating an assist, but she figured she'd helped on at least two enemies.

She needed over twenty thousand points to even begin to get into the league of the top dogs around this world. Which meant...hundreds of kills. If she could manage two a day, she'd be at this for a year just to get through the first world.

"Any other ways to get points?" she asked.

"Sometimes," Harald said slowly. "Those dungeons and quest areas the others mentioned earlier? They can give a lot of realm points. But they're usually insanely tough to beat. They're more like a raid than an old-school dungeon."

Sam stared at him blankly.

"And you don't understand a word of that, do you?" he asked.

She shook her head.

"You'll learn as you go," he replied. "Right now, we need

to get moving. Lord Siggund owns this keep. We're joining his forces to attack Klaastaad Faste. It's a Red keep."

Blue, green, now red. "How many factions are there?" she asked.

"Five. Blue, green, red, yellow, black." They'd reached the courtyard. Harald raised his voice to an echoing holler. "Rally up!"

Men and women alike rushed to grab their weapons and move out into the court. Sam took a moment to snag another handful of the healing herbs as she went for her weapons and shield. The stuff tasted like raw oregano, but it seemed to work.

You have eaten healing herbs! Your health will recover at plus two points per minute for the next ten minutes!

As effective as it was, she grabbed another little bundle of it and stashed it in her pouch with the coins she had. That reminded her... There had to be a way to keep things beyond death. She didn't want to start with nothing, if she came back in a bad way after today's battles. Harald seemed to be busy organizing his troop, so she went to ask Alwyn instead.

"Is there a way to store things?" Sam asked. "You know, in case?"

"Sure," Alwyn replied. "Olaf's shop hooks up to the shops in all the other keeps we control, and the castle as well. You can leave coin with him and it's accessible at any faction base. Items are harder. You can only stow items at the Bank, which is at Blarkastali."

Sam gave her a blank look.

"Our home castle," Alwyn supplied. "Literally, 'Castle Blue' in old Norse."

"OK, that makes sense. I'm going to stash this coin then.

Just in case," Sam said.

"Hurry!"

She dashed off to Olaf's and opened an account there. It was a simple enough interface. A popup screen appeared in her vision, and she deposited the coins into the system there. When she checked her purse, they were gone. It worked well enough, she supposed.

Jogging back toward the troop, she found herself growing irritated with the whole thing. If this were just a game, she could see herself having a decent time in this world. Even come to enjoy it after a while, maybe. The camaraderie was comfortingly familiar. The fighting was exciting and interesting. She'd met some nice people, and she was truly growing to like Harald and Alwyn.

But even though all that was true, this wasn't her life. She had a world to get back to, parents who would be missing her. A workplace that was going to go looking for her. She hadn't been missing for a full twenty-four hours yet. At least in game time. Did the virtual days run at the same pace as the real world outside? Sam sighed in frustration. There was so damned much she didn't know about this place.

That lack of knowledge was slowing down her escape from Valhalla Online. To get out of there, she needed to learn as much as she could, as fast as she could. Somehow she needed to separate herself from the crowd, break away and win a hell of a lot more Realm Points than most others were. Harald said that owning a keep — and holding it — was a thousand points a day. If she could learn from him how that was done during this raid, Sam could slash the time required a ton.

The gates opened as Sam took her place in line. She stayed close to Harald. If she was going to learn how to capture one of these keeps for herself, she needed to be close by his side for this attack. Together they marched out of Blendrake Faste and off to war.

13

Sam heaved, helping another warrior shove a ladder against the wall. He took an arrow in the shoulder and jerked away, grunting. The sudden shift of the weight almost tore the ladder from Sam's grasp, but she held on. Gritting her teeth, she leaned in against it and it slammed home against the wall.

"I've got you covered!" Alwyn shouted. She had her bow in her hands and was loosing arrow after arrow against the defenders up on the wall.

Her spear wasn't going to be much use on the ladder. Sam discarded it at the bottom and drew the axe from her belt. She kept her shield raised high as best she could and started climbing. Harald had already led a squad up another pair of ladders, but the enemy had managed to dislodge both ladders, and Harald's people were outnumbered on the wall. If they couldn't even the odds quickly, the whole attack might fail.

An arrow struck Sam's shield, shuddering as it thudded into the wood. There was a scream from up on the wall.

"Got him for you. Keep going!" Alwyn shouted from below.

Sam looked back over her shoulder. More of Harald's men were behind her on the ladder. They climbed grimly, wordlessly, ducked down behind their own shields. She turned back toward the top and began ascending again.

Somehow she made the top. A sword clattered against her shield and she lashed out with it blindly, connecting with something. She pushed off against the ladder with her legs and climbed over the rampart as fast as she could, facing off immediately with a swordsman who was bleeding heavily from his nose. Her shield must have struck his face. While he was still stunned from the blow, she slashed low with her axe. It bit into his leg and he fell to the floor howling.

Pain here was diminished, not absent. The feel of having an axe tear into the inside of a thigh couldn't be much fun. She stepped over the fallen man. Ahead of her were the red troops pinning Harald's people down. Their backs were turned to her. She grinned at the two men who climbed quietly over the wall to stand beside her.

With a shout all three of them tore into the rear ranks of the red fighters. It was a slaughter. Harald's men pushed from the other side, and Sam's people took them from behind. In moments the enemy had been completely cut down.

Sam checked her stats quickly.

Health 26/30, Stamina 22/100, Mana 0/0.

She'd gotten a slice on her right arm somewhere during the battle, and she was darned near out of stamina. Between the climb and the fight, she was feeling worn out. Her breath was coming in fast gasps.

"Need to do more running," she said.

"Come on," Harald growled. "To the inner keep. Most of their people are away. We can take this thing together if we move before they react!"

Sam followed in his wake, descending the stairs into the courtyard. More guards waited for them there, six burly fighters in armor. These defenders were new to her. They didn't look like the ones she'd fought before. All were clad in the same red mail, bearing identical swords and shields. In fact, it looked like they all had the same ruddy beards on their faces.

"They're not players, just computer controlled MOBs," Alwyn shouted to her. "Tough but slow. Surround them. I'll hit them with arrows from the stairs!"

She made good on her plan while she was shouting, firing an arrow into the nearest guard. He staggered back as the dart stabbed through the links in his mail. Sam slashed in at a knee that was sticking out from beneath its shield and connected, but there was hardened leather there as well. Her blade didn't bite very deep.

You've hit the Red Guard for 3 damage.

How much health did these things have? In response to the question, a new bar appeared on the left side of her vision, tracking the guard's health. She couldn't see a number, but she watched the meter slowly trickle down as more fighters surrounded it and hacked away.

The guard lashed out with his sword, decapitating the man standing beside Sam. The attack left an opening under his arm though, and she hammered a blow into the weak spot.

Critical hit! You've hit the Red Guard for 12 damage!

He turned his attention on her. An arrow stabbed into its shoulder, but he kept coming. She backed away a step, raising her shield to try to block the inevitable attack. Sam managed to take the sword swing on her shield, but the blow shattered the wood frame completely and threw her backward into the dirt.

Sam tossed the useless bits away and rolled to one side, dodging the next sword swing. More arrows sprouted from the guard, and he staggered under the attack. Then an axe blow hammered into the guard's shoulder. The guard reeled under the blow. The axe rose and descended another time, shattering the opposite shoulder. As wordlessly as he had fought, the guard fell to the ground.

Harald stood on the other side of the guard, removing his axe from its shoulder. He offered Sam his hand. "Ready to finish this?"

She took his arm and hauled herself back to her feet. "I'm with you."

They stormed through the doors into the keep. It looked just like the one she'd had breakfast in this morning. All the keeps seemed to be nearly identical, although the outer walls were laid out a bit differently for each. The banners were different here – red blazons hanging from the walls, instead of blue. At the far end of the hall rose a fire just like the one Sam had bound to this morning.

But beside that fire stood a massive figure in red armor. This wasn't mail, either. The armor was made of overlapping steel plates. As she looked, Sam could see glimpses of mail beneath. She wasn't even sure how her axe was going to cut through that stuff. He was armed with a massive longsword and a huge shield of some gleaming silvery metal.

Harald never paused, though. He strode forward, axe up at the ready. The red commander met him halfway across the room and the battle was joined. They rained down blow after blow on each other. The commander's armor protected him from most of the furious wrath Harald's axe attempted to exact. For his part Harald dodged out of the way of most of his opponent's blows. Sam saw more than one sword swing strike home though, and Harald was tiring as well.

He wasn't alone, though. Alwyn launched arrows into the commander. Most simply bounced off his plate armor, but one stuck into a joint near the left shoulder. The other warriors circled the commander, stabbing and thrusting in with their weapons. Slowly they wore him down, one small cut at a time.

Harald maintained his attention. Every time the commander tried to attack another warrior Harald would strike him somewhere, turning himself into the main target again. The battle seemed to continue forever. Sam's arms were burning with the effort of keeping her axe moving. She didn't have the energy left to see how much stamina she had remaining, but it had to be just about none.

Then all at once Harald gave a mighty roar. He stepped in close to the warrior, his axe suddenly glowing with a brilliant blue light. The weapon sizzled as it sliced through the air, striking the commander's neck with explosive force. A boom sounded throughout the hall, and there was a flash like lightning.

When Sam could see again, the red commander had fallen to the ground, headless. The battle was over.

Harald looked more tired than Sam had ever seen him. He was bleeding from countless wounds. But he smiled as he slowly unrolled a clenched fist, revealing a sparkling red gem. Harald strode to the hearth-fire. He glanced over his shoulder, making eye contact with Sam. She nodded back to him. This was how it was done. This was how a keep was taken. He was showing her the way, and she observed his every move carefully.

He stood before the flame and cast the gem in. It flashed blue. All around the hall, the banners — which had been red — rolled themselves up. When they unrolled again they were blue.

"And that is how you take a keep," Harald said. "Well done, all. Rest a while. The enemy will want it back, and we must see if we can hold the place now that we've won it."

Sam sat herself down on the floor of the keep, more tired than she'd ever been before. She'd seen how to win a keep, true enough. But she couldn't imagine ever being strong enough to battle a commander the way Harald had. There was no easy route to victory for her, no simple path to the Realm Points she needed. For the first time she admitted to herself that she might well be stuck in this place for a lot longer than she'd hoped.

14

Looting bodies was one of the strangest experiences of this new world. The idea of basically going through someone's pockets for loose change, stripping off their armor, and grabbing any other valuables they had was completely alien to Sam. It helped a little that the game changed the fallen shortly after death. Living beings bled, and cried out in pain. But a short while after dying, the bodies lost some of their personalization. The facial features went vague, flow of blood stopped, and the bodies themselves took on a more plastic appearance. She supposed that was to help people like herself get over feeling squeamish about robbing dead bodies. The result felt more like stripping clothes off fallen mannequins.

Sam picked up a sword dropped by a fallen warrior. As effective as her axe had been in the last battle, she was beginning to appreciate that the sword might just be more useful for her. The stabbing point was better at finding weak spots in armor, and the heavy blade was almost as good at breaking apart shields as her axe.

She sheathed the sword and belted it around her waist.

The game system notified her that she had acquired an 'iron sword', and that she lacked the skill to use it. She'd have to learn, if she wanted to be effective with the thing. Maybe Alwyn could work with her to acquire the skill.

The loot distribution in this raid was much more a free-for-all than it had been when Harald had controlled distribution. He'd pooled everything, doled out useful items where they were needed, sold the rest, and distributed the spoils. His people trusted him to do that, but his band of warriors only numbered about a score of the fifty remaining after the attack was done.

The result was something of a mess. A few blue warriors were already stripping valuables off their dead foes before the commander was defeated. Siggund and Harald put a stop to that right away. But what followed wasn't much different, with people rushing about clearing away anything of value from their fallen foes then selling it to the shop as quickly as they could.

Sam wrapped up the things she'd collected from this body in the dead man's cloak and hauled the mess over to the vendor. As she staggered on under her load, Alwyn dashed past her, dragging her own cloak-load on the ground behind her.

"What's the rush?" Sam asked.

"Got to grab while we can," Alwyn said. "The reds will counterattack. If we have to retreat, anything we haven't snagged will be lost."

"How soon will they come?"

"Could be any time now," Alwyn said with a shrug.

Sam dumped her load on the counter. This shop was run by a woman who said her name was Brenda. She had the broad smile and somewhat vacant look that by now Sam recognized meant she was a computer controlled character, not a player. An interface appeared in her vision and she began transferring items over to the store, while the coins she got back in return tallied up in a little bar at the bottom. She wasn't making as much from this fight as she had with Harald's team, but it would help. She deposited the entire amount into her bank once the sale was complete. No sense carrying around wealth where it could be lost.

She looked around the courtyard. The looting was about done. About half of the warriors were milling about or heading into the great hall for lunch. Others were picking over the last of their fallen foes. At first she didn't see Harald, but Sam finally spotted him. He stood alone on the north wall, staring out into the distance.

Sam went up the stairs to stand beside him. He didn't say anything, and for a few minutes she held her peace as well. She looked out over the forest, wondering what he was doing. Was there something out there that she just wasn't seeing? Finally, her patience simply wore out.

"What are you looking for?" she asked.

"The enemy," he replied. "This fort was won too damned easily. Where are the other reds? Why weren't they here? Why haven't they counterattacked yet?"

He glared at her as if he was demanding some sort of answer from her. Sam didn't have one for him, and shrugged.

"You know these people better than I do," she said. "If their troops aren't coming here, then they have to be somewhere else, right? Where would they be striking?"

An alert displayed across Sam's vision. From the startled look on Harald's face, she could tell that he had gotten the same message.

Blendrake Faste has been captured by the enemy! Your bind-point has been changed to Blarkastali.

"Well, now we know where the enemy was," Harald said. "Damn it. Siggund! We need to talk!"

A burly man in the court below nodded. "Coming up."

Siggund took the steps up to the wall two at a time, loping along with long legs that were so thick they reminded Sam of tree trunks. He had a massive beard which matched his enormous frame. Dressed in a mail tunic that covered his arms down to his wrists and draped over his thighs, he also had a massive sword belted to his waist.

"Took my fort, they did," Siggund said. "The bastards."

"We'll get it back," Harald replied.

"Not if we're fighting from the castle, we won't. Not easily. They push us all the way back and we'll be penned in there. The other factions will all coordinate to ensure we have a damned hard time breaking out."

"Which is why this keep just became important. The last thing we want is for Thorsten to control the last blue fort," Harald said.

"He'd never let us hear the end of it," Siggund said with a dark chuckle.

Sam kept silent, listening to the two discuss strategy. The loss of Blendrake was more than an inconvenience. It sounded like it could devastate the overall efforts of their faction. That was bad for her, since anything that made it harder for them all to win keeps would make it more difficult for her to earn the Realm Points she needed.

As she listened, she also scanned the wood line. Harald's warning that the enemy would come on them soon was as important as ever. He was distracted, discussing strategy with Siggund, but she was still free to keep an eye on the woods. At first, she thought the rustling movement she saw was only the wind moving through the trees. Sam quickly realized that it was the movement of troops. Many troops. A veritable horde of warriors was coming their way.

"Harald!" she said. "They're here."

He moved to the wall beside her, scanning the oncoming wave as they broke from the forest. "To the walls! We are attacked!"

All around them the castle exploded into action. Warriors raced to the wall top. Alwyn was there before most of the others, a fresh quiver of arrows at her side. She drew and loosed her first shot. Someone in the cleared space between the woods and the fort cried out in pain, and she was already nocking another arrow. But there were so many of them.

"Red and green working together," Siggund growled. "No wonder they took Blendrake so quickly.

"They have the numbers, for sure. But we can hold this place, if we work together," Harald said.

"I'm with you," Siggund said. The men clasped arms.

Sam heard a cry of alarm from the other side of the wall, and then a cheer. She looked over and saw another force breaking from the woods. This one wore blue. Reinforcements! With additional troops, they ought to be able to win the day. She was about to add her own voice to the cheering when she heard Harald mutter something under his breath.

"He wouldn't dare," Siggund said.

"This is Thorsten," Harald said. "He'd dare a lot to hurt me."

The cheers from the other wall turned into a cry of pain and then shouts of alarm. One of the men standing there had been shot by an arrow. It hadn't been enough to kill him, but the shaft stuck from his arm, and he fell backward to hide behind the ramparts as more arrows flew toward the defenders there.

Thorsten hadn't come to help them. He'd come to help the enemy, and the hell with the damage it did to his own faction. Sam was pretty sure the politics involved were deeper than she knew, but she couldn't help but think that her disregard of his commands the day before had helped inspire this. Maybe he would have gone down this road anyway. Or maybe seeing even newcomers to the world side with Harald over him had tipped Thorsten over the edge.

Whatever the cause, he'd brought another several score warriors to the battle. Sam had a feeling that would be more than enough to turn a difficult battle into one that was impossible to win.

15

Alwyn kept shooting, but she was running short on arrows. Another warrior sprinted down the stairs to the shop to purchase more for her. She and the other half dozen archers were the best defense they had, at this point. Once the enemy had ladders against the walls and began to climb, they'd have their hands full and then some. Sam glanced at the warriors they had in place. There weren't enough. Not to hold all four walls against a force this size.

To make things even worse, she saw why the mixed green and red army was moving so slowly. They had a massive battering ram with them, making its rumbling way slowly out of the woods.

Seeing that, Harald strode to the edge of the wall, glaring down at the thing. He raised his left hand toward the sky. With his right hand he traced something in the air. Light flashed in his palm, and then shot forward toward the men around the ram. It struck and blasted several of them into the air.

That only slowed the weapon a little, though. Others

quickly ran forward to take up the positions of their fallen friends. The ram rumbled into movement once more. Harald shook his fist angrily.

"Can you do that again?" Sam asked him.

"Not often enough to make a difference against so many," Harald said. "I'll save my mana for when it will do more good."

She wanted to ask him what he had done. Wanted to ask so many more questions about a wild variety of things. There was still so much she didn't know about this world.

But she did know people. She had a good feel for the sort of man Thorsten was, and because she understood how he thought she was pretty sure she knew how to disable his force completely. If only for a little while.

"If Thorsten wasn't here, could you win this fight?" she asked.

"Maybe. It would be close, but we'd have a good chance," he said. "It doesn't matter though. He is here. Not much is going to turn him away from getting back at me. If you're hoping to appeal to his heart, he doesn't have one."

"I'm hoping to embarrass the hell out of him in front of his men," Sam said. "He's got to be mad about my violating his commands."

"Yes, but not enough to turn away."

"Leave that part to me. If I can get out there, and then get him to follow me with his force, can you beat the others?" Sam asked. She was shaking a little at the thought. Having fifty or so angry armed men chasing her through the woods would be a nightmare. She was pretty sure the worst they could do to her was kill her, though. In Valhalla, that didn't matter much. She hoped there wasn't anything more that they could do, anyway.

She swallowed back the fear. This was the only way she

could help. She wasn't going to let Thorsten undermine her chances of success.

"Yes, we can beat them," Harald said. "If they catch you, it won't be pleasant."

"I'll try to make sure they don't," she said.

"There's a postern gate you can use. Dump anything extra. One weapon and a shield."

Sam held up the shield she was carrying, and nodded toward the sword at her belt. "These will do."

"Can you even use that thing?" Harald asked her, looking at the sword. "Don't answer that. Come here, you'll need a few things for this to have a chance in Hel of working."

Harald touched her gently on the shoulder. An icon appeared in her vision. She looked at it, and it expanded in her view.

Congratulations! You have learned the skill 'Sword'! The pointy end goes in the other guy!

Congratulations! You have learned the skill 'Running'! He who fights and runs away...

Congratulations! You have learned the skill 'Endurance'! Your stamina will recover more quickly.

He paused for just a moment, then touched her again, adding a fourth skill.

Congratulations! You have learned the skill 'Rune Binding'! The mystic powers of the runes are yours to command.

"What does that mean?" Sam asked.

"Nothing until you learn some runes as well," Harald replied. "It's a rare skill, and my way of saying thank you for your courage. Come see me once all this is over. No matter how it ends. I'll work with you some more, teach you the basics of magic."

That sounded promising. If she had her pistol with her, this whole mess would be a very different story. Thorsten's lightning bolt magic had to be some of the rune-magic he was talking about. Having that sort of power at her disposal would feel a lot like carrying a pistol on her hip.

"Thank you," she said. "For everything."

"Thank you," he rumbled in reply. "You'd best go now if you want to get clear in time. There's a small postern door you can use to get away near the wall Thorsten is approaching. I'll show you the way."

They hurried down the stairs, through the courtyard to a back corner near the keep that Sam hadn't noticed before. A massive door was set there, girded with iron bars.

"Shouldn't you be on the wall? Sam asked.

"I'm the only one who can open this door," he said. "It's a sally port. It can be broken from the outside — with difficulty. But only I or someone I appoint can open it otherwise. I haven't had time to set up keep officers to spread the duty around."

He placed his hand on the door, and she heard a click. The door opened freely now, revealing a short passage through the wall to yet another door. Murder holes on either side would make the breaking of the second door a truly brutal experience for any attackers. Harald ushered her in, entered himself, and then shut the door behind them. Then he repeated the process on the outer door.

"Have to be certain no one gets in," he said. "A strike from behind would be devastating."

She nodded her understanding. Adrenaline was kicking in now. She was breathing faster, her limbs feeling full of energy. She was going to need all of that energy in another minute or two. Harald unlocked the outer door and opened it cautiously. He peered outside, but none of the enemy had gotten near enough to be a threat yet.

"Go quickly, and good luck," he said. He reached out a hand to her. She took it, clasping it in her own.

"Thanks. I'll need it!" she replied. Then in a flash, she was out through the door and moving away from the fort as quickly as she could.

Sam dashed across the rough ground, running through the dry moat that surrounded the place. She was headed straight toward the blue force led by Thorsten. She'd made some serious claims inside, and she wondered now if she was actually going to be able to convince Thorsten to follow her rather than attack the keep. Everything would depend on her getting under his skin.

That she was hopeful that she could manage. Getting away afterward was gonna be a lot harder.

16

Sam charged straight toward the oncoming blue battle group. She kept her shield up, but she was pretty sure they weren't going to shoot her without finding out who she was first. After all, she was wearing their color too. For all they knew she was a scout, rushing back to report to Thorsten about the keep's defenses.

You'd need to be utterly mad to rush an enemy force all by yourself. Which was precisely what she was doing, but her gut said that she could pull this off if she played her cards just right.

She knew people. That had always been one of her biggest assets. Sam had been interested in combat arms, in fighting on the line with the infantry or armor, back when she'd first arrived at West Point. It wasn't until she'd spent a couple of months tailing behind a military police investigator that she'd really found her calling, though.

Sam watched all through that summer as Captain Clarke — the officer she'd been detailed to work with — wrung confessions out of people she never thought would talk. He'd been able to somehow know what they were thinking. Or feeling, maybe. He'd used that knowledge to manipulate them into falling right into his carefully laid traps. It was like martial arts, but with words instead of fists. Sam loved it. She'd delved into the work upon her return to the academy, studying everything she could about psychology and criminology. It had been easy getting an MP appointment.

Now she was applying those skills in a new venue. Thorsten was easy. He swung his power around like a club, beating down anyone who dared stand against him. That stemmed from an inherent sense of fear. He was terrified that someone was going to find him out, that one of his people would learn he was a fraud and call him on it. Everything he did was motivated by his insecurity.

In her hands, that was a weapon.

She was close enough that the front ranks were taking notice of her approach, but they still weren't peppering her with arrows yet. That was a plus. She needed to be close enough to Thorsten for him to hear her.

"Halt!" One of the men in the lead ranks shouted out to her. He had raised his spear.

She didn't slow down. Shield leveled at the man, Sam barreled ahead. His weapon licked out toward her but glanced off the surface of her shield. She kept her center of gravity low as she crashed into him. He was bowled over backward and she stepped past him. Her sword licked out and sliced deep into an exposed thigh as she passed.

Now they'd identified her as an enemy, but the troop didn't seem to know quite what to do with her. They had no idea who she was, but she must be someone important and powerful if she was charging a large band like that by herself. They hesitated, and then locked shields into a wall formation. The wall was like a hedgehog, bristling with spear points and sword blades. If she closed with that she'd be dead in an instant. Luckily, she didn't need to close with them to achieve her goal.

"Where is Thorsten?" she called out in a parade-ground voice that would have made any Drill Sergeant proud. "Where is that toad-licking piece of shit that leads good warriors against their allies? Where is the cowardly soup-sandwich that allies himself with the Greens and Reds over his fellow Blues?"

The line held its formation. They didn't approach her, but they didn't back down either. Sam all but held her breath while at the same time trying to appear as fierce and powerful as possible. If they saw how badly her knees wanted to shake, they'd be all over her in a heartbeat.

"Girl, get the hell out of our way," Thorsten said. He stepped around the side of his formation, coming into view. "We're here for that bastard Harald, not you. Run along like a good little girl."

There were chuckles in the shield wall at his words, and they began to advance on her again. One of them threw a spear her way. Sam side-stepped and it missed, stabbing into the soil where she'd been standing. She needed to do something more to stop them.

"I may just be a girl, Thorsten, but I defied you yesterday," Sam hollered back. "I defy you today. I will defy you tomorrow as well, and for a hundred hundred tomorrows to come as well. You are nothing. You are dirt. You do not deserve your rank or title."

Then she whirled, sheathing her sword as she spun and scooped the spear out of the ground where it lay. She finished the motion and set herself, letting her body think that this was just a javelin, and she was back at West Point getting ready to throw for competition. She threw the spear.

It hurtled through the air toward Thorsten. He brought his shield up just in time to stop the weapon. The spearhead punched through the wood, shattering the shield. He dropped the defense and shook his arm, droplets of blood spattering from the limb. She'd hurt him! The blow had been a lucky shot. Sam doubted that she could repeat that if she tried again a dozen times. These spears didn't have the same weight as a collegiate competition javelin. She'd need a lot of practice to get good at throwing them.

But she'd wounded Thorsten. Now she could see it there in his eyes, that fear she sensed in him the other day. The raw terror underneath his bullying exterior shell. He was afraid that someone just like her would show everyone what he really was.

"I name you coward, Thorsten," Sam said. Her voice was level but pitched to carry.

"Kill her," Thorsten said. It was barely more than a whisper at first. But the pink of his cheeks brightened into full red, and he said it again and again, his voice louder each time. "Kill her. Kill her!"

That did it. The shield wall set themselves and marched forward in earnest now. Behind them archers took aim and fired a pair of arrows at Sam. She ducked behind her own shield. The darts slammed into the wood with a series of sharp thuds.

"Can't do it yourself, Thorsten?" Sam taunted. She drew her sword again, backing away from the line of men coming at her. "Have to have them do the work for you?"

"I don't need help from anyone to deal with you!" he growled. He tossed aside his broken shield and drew a pair of axes from his belt. Then he started toward Sam, his long strides eating up the ground.

That was what she'd been waiting for. Sam twisted

around and bolted away from Thorsten. She ducked between two trees. He was too large and had to go around. It gave her a little bit of a head start, and she used it to lead him and his men away from the keep as fast as her legs could carry her.

Behind her Sam heard Thorsten bellowing at her with incoherent rage. She'd definitely found the right buttons to push. His entire troop had given up on their shield wall and were following along behind them.

"Too slow, too big, too clumsy," Sam yelled back at Thorsten. His outraged growl was about ten feet behind her now. Sam put on another little burst of speed. The ground was slanting up here, the forest thinning out. She couldn't find any more small patches that she could dart through and make Thorsten go around. Already her stamina was halfway down. She figured he likely had a lot more of it to burn than she did.

How long had she bought Harald so far? She guessed that the delay had been ten, maybe fifteen minutes tops. Another five or ten for them to march back to the keep. It wasn't enough. She needed to win Harald at least a little more time.

"Now who's the coward?" Thorsten asked her. "Why are you running?"

"Because you smell awful," Sam shouted back. There was a cave up ahead. Maybe she could hole up in there, find a spot in the back that she could tuck herself into and evade him and his men. She sprinted for the cave as hard as she could.

Sam had almost made it to the opening when a sharp pain stabbed into her left shoulder. The impact threw her face-first into the leaves. Neither the blow nor the fall really hurt as much as they should have, but her visual display showed that half of her health had vanished with that one attack. Looking back at the wound, Sam saw the feathered end of an arrow shaft protruding from her.

Beyond that, just a stone's throw away, were Thorsten and his men. They charged.

17

Sam groaned, trying to force herself back to her feet. It wasn't that she was hurting too badly to rise. She'd fought through worse than this. But the combination of the injury with her low stamina was taking a toll on this virtual body she inhabited.

Get the hell up and keep going, she could almost hear her old mentor tell her. *The job demands everything you can give it, every day, no matter where you are.*

Even here, she wondered? If Clarke found himself lost in this virtual world, would he keep going? What would he do?

The very first thing he would do would be to get up. She stood, scrambling to her feet as another arrow stabbed into the dirt to her left. Then Sam was dashing forward again, making for the dubious shelter of the cave. She couldn't tell from the outside how deep the place was, but it had to be better than out there getting cut to ribbons by Thorsten and his goons.

She ducked inside. The cave ceiling was about twelve feet above her head, and the cave extended back into darkness. Sam kept going, staggering against one wall with the effort of staying on her feet. There didn't seem to be any place in here to hide, but if it was deep enough maybe she could just lose herself in the darkness.

Sam could feel blood running down her back. On the corner of her screen was a tiny icon showing that she was bleeding, her health continuing to leak away. She was down to a third of her health now, and it was still dropping. If she couldn't bind the wound soon, she'd die of that one arrow shot.

Torches flashed into light on either side of the passage. Sam blinked, and a message appeared in her vision.

You have discovered the Ruins of Kaladesh. This place was once a dwarf citadel, ages past. It fell to dark enemies, and has been long lost. This is a mandatory bind dungeon. If you proceed beyond this point you will be spirit bound to this place until you change your bind point. Do you wish to proceed? Y/N

What did that mean? Bind here? Sam's thinking was growing fuzzy from the blood loss. She touched her shoulder. The arrow was still embedded there. Behind her she heard the clatter of warriors entering the cave. They were following her in, coming after her even into this place. Damn it all, she had to have bought Harald enough time at this point. She ought to just let them kill her, but something about the idea still unsettled her. Sam didn't want to just die. It was like giving up. A surrender that she just couldn't bring herself to make.

She tried to stagger forward again, but something stopped her. There was an invisible barrier across the passage. The message flashed in her vision again.

Do you wish to proceed? Y/N

What had the others said about binding and dungeons? Something about them being dangerous, but she couldn't recall precisely why. Sam's thoughts tumbled together. The enemy would be on her any second, though. She had to keep moving, get away from them somehow.

"Yes, I want to proceed, damn it," she muttered.

The barrier vanished and she half walked, half stumbled forward a few more steps. Two more torches lit her way, showing her that the cave walls were becoming smoother, and that the passage was angling down.

"Why haven't you idiots killed her yet?" Thorsten called from somewhere behind her.

Sam turned and saw four men and two women milling about in the middle of the passage. Something was stopping them in their tracks. That barrier! It had allowed Sam to pass through, but not Thorsten's men? Why?

"Lord Thorsten, it's a bind dungeon," one of the men said. "It won't let us by unless we bind here."

"It let her through, though? That means she's bound here," Thorsten said. He walked right up to the barrier and stopped in his tracks. "Shoot her, then."

Two archers lined up. Sam looked around for cover, but there was none to be had. She ducked behind her shield, using it to block the first volley of arrows that streaked her way, and then the second. The shield trembled with each hit. The worst of it was that the shield wasn't big enough to cover her entire body, even crouched down behind it. Sooner or later one of the arrows would strike home.

"Wait!" Thorsten said. "I have a better idea for this troublesome bitch. Everyone out of the cave."

A long pause went by before Sam dared to peek up from behind her shield. They were gone. Thorsten and all his men were nowhere to be seen. At first, she thought it was just a trick, and she hesitated a moment before rising to her feet. Even then she was as careful as she could be, stalking forward slowly, shield and sword at the ready.

Sam passed the spot where the barrier had been. It didn't seem to block her anymore. That was because she'd bound here. She recalled Alwyn's advice on binding at last. If she was bound here and died, she'd come back here tomorrow morning. Without her gear, without her weapons or armor. She'd have to make the run to the nearest blue keep to recover anything at all.

Then the ground shook, throwing her to the floor. Rocks and dust fell from the ceiling. She covered her head with her arms. She'd never been in an earthquake before, but this had to be what it was like. There was a terrible grinding noise, like the earth was tearing itself in half. The stones around her groaned and she thought the entire cave was about to collapse upon itself.

It held. More small rocks pattered down on her arms and back, but the cave itself remained structurally intact. When everything had at last settled down, and even the dust had begun drifting back toward the floor, Sam raised her head again.

The character of the light had changed. She stepped down the hall, not realizing at first what had happened. But then she came to the spot where the entrance to the cave should have been. It wasn't there anymore. Instead there was a massive pile of rocks, gravel, and boulders. Somehow Thorsten had collapsed the entrance to the cave. He'd sealed her inside.

It took a few minutes for the implications of that entrapment to sink into Sam's wound-clouded mind. She'd spirit bound herself to this place, so if she died she would respawn inside the cave. And the only exit from the cave that she knew of had been utterly blocked off. She was trapped in this place, and if she couldn't find another way out she might spend forever dying and coming back, imprisoned within a virtual cave in a virtual world for all time.

18

Survival first. She could figure out the rest later. Her first step had to be making sure she didn't immediately die from her wound. Sure, she'd eventually respawn here, but what if her friends came looking for her in the meantime? Sam was sure they would eventually seek her out. With luck the time she'd bought Harald had been enough. If his force had knocked back the red and green armies, then Thorsten would likely retreat. He wasn't the sort to come against a ready foe in anything close to an even battle.

No, he'd bide his time. Sam was confident she had Harald's measure as well. He would come looking for her. She stared at the pile of boulders hopelessly. Even if he found her, how could he move all that? She remembered his lightning bolts, the magic he'd called down from the skies. Thorsten must have some sort of similar power over the earth. That must have been how he caused the collapse. Maybe Harald could use his own magic to free her.

"Until then, I need to stay alive," she said. Which meant solving the bleeding issue. She could barely see the arrow, but it needed to come out. She broke off the shaft and then pushed the arrowhead the rest of the way through her shoulder.

There was no way she could have done that, if the pain had been real. As it was, the feeling was one of the strangest and least pleasant she'd ever faced. Her mind was telling her that the pain was similar to pulling out a bad splinter. Her fingers were telling her that she was sliding something the size of her thumb out through loops of shoulder muscle.

Sam was exhausted by the time she finished the job. She tore off a strip of cloth from her shirt to slow the bleeding. For good measure she took the healing herbs that she'd stuffed in her pouch earlier and ate half of them, using the other half as a poultice for the wound. The ache eased almost as soon as the herbs touched the injury, and she sighed with relief.

The wound bound, she found her eyes closing. Her stamina was recovering a little, her blood loss had stopped, and she still had a couple of health points left. The exhaustion was as much emotional as it was physical. She'd been chased by people trying to hurt her and trapped in a dark place all alone.

"I've got a right to be tired," she said, letting her eyelids droop a bit.

She woke some time later. There was no telling how long she'd been out. Without a watch or even the sky to tell the time of day, she might have slept for minutes or hours. She checked her stats.

Health 23/30, Stamina 100/100, Mana 50/50.

She'd been out for a while then, for her health to recover so far. Not a full night of rest, but hours at least. Sam grunted as she rolled back to her feet. Her left shoulder was sore, but she could move it freely again. She yanked the arrows from her shield. It was still serviceable, if a little banged up. Her sword was still there by her hip. If trouble came, she was at least a little ready for it.

Sam's stomach was beginning to growl, though. Could you starve to death in this game? No one carried rations during their raids on the keeps. Sam had never seen anyone carry food around out there. But there seemed to be an unlimited supply at the banquet hall in every keep, ready for warriors to eat whenever they grew hungry. However long she'd been down here, lunch was definitely a while ago.

Food and water were going to be a serious issue if she ended up stuck in this place for very long.

Maybe she could find supplies deeper in the cave. The display had said that this place was an ancient dwarf home, abandoned a long time ago. Sam didn't think any food they'd left behind would still be edible, but if they had a water supply it might still be viable.

She walked down the passage, passing the two sets of torches. Sam was half expecting another set of torches to blaze to light when she reached the outer edge of their glow, but none did. It seemed like four torches might be all she got from the place. She went back to the nearest one and looked at it.

The torch was a wooden handle the size of a child's baseball bat, capped with a metal cup. The thing wasn't burning, not really. It glowed with a pale light that came from something set inside the hollow at the tip. Sam wasn't sure what the glowing stuff was, but it wasn't on fire. She ran her hand through the 'flame' experimentally and it wasn't even warm.

It came loose from the wall easily enough, though. She could carry one of the things with her to light her way as she explored. She went forward with the torch in her right hand, her shield in her left.

The cave continued forward at a slight angle down. It was descending deeper, toward what she couldn't imagine. Several times the flickering light case shadows on the walls which made her start. Each time Sam considered going back. If Harald came for her when she was too deep, she'd never know it. But hunger and the fear that he never would come drove her onward.

None of them had any idea where she was, after all. Thorsten and some of his people knew, but somehow Sam didn't think they were likely to help Harald find her. Harald would have no idea she was trapped here at all. Worst case, he'd figure she was back at the blue castle.

"I've gotten myself into this mess. It's going to be up to me to get myself out of it," she said softly.

The sound of her voice seemed to be eaten up by the gloomy darkness just outside her torchlight. Then all at once there was a glint from up ahead, the flash of a reflection that looked like light glancing off steel. She froze, but didn't see the light again.

"Is someone there?" Sam called out.

There was no answer.

Sam shifted the torch to the same hand as the shield. It was ungainly carrying both items in her left hand, but she wanted the right hand free. She drew her sword and moved on down the passage.

The shining she had seen was light reflecting off a door. It was smaller than the passage, only about five feet in height, but almost as wide as it was tall. The door was bound with heavy iron hinges. A knocker was set into the door. Sam couldn't see any way to open it.

"Am I supposed to knock?" she asked the air incredulously.

There was no answer, but she hadn't been expecting one. She reached out and touched the knocker, rapping it sharply against the wood once. The knock gave a hollow booming sound that seemed to carry like a drum-beat. The door creaked slowly open a few inches.

"Well, that was easy enough," she said.

She pushed the door open the rest of the way and stepped inside. The room inside was the size of a basketball court. Columns reached up from the floor to a vaulted ceiling overhead that was high enough her torchlight barely reflected off it at all. Before she could do more than glance around the room, a gleaming blade flashed toward her ribs. Sam cried out with alarm and parried the blow with her shield.

A small green humanoid stood before her, all scales and warped features. It screeched in a high-pitched voice that hurt her ears. The thing held a wicked dagger in one hand, and even as she took in its uncanny appearance it used the weapon to stab at her again.

19

Sam brought her shield up, blocking the dagger strike a second time. The thing squealed again, rushing at her. She dropped the torch. It clattered to the floor, spinning and bouncing after it landed. The light sent crazy shadows careening off the walls and ceiling.

Without the torch, Sam had better control over her shield. She slammed it down against the creature's weapon arm. The dagger flew from its hand, rebounding off the wall.

"I don't want to hurt you," Sam said. What was this thing? This couldn't be a player. Nobody would choose to live in this sort of form. That meant this had to be a computer controlled character. It would only have the motivations that were programmed into it. Unlike the uploaded humans, it would be immune to manipulation, and only open to negotiation if its code allowed it to be.

It backed away from her. For a moment Sam thought that it would flee, now that it was disarmed. She let the tip of her sword drop a little. Not enough to really let her guard down, but enough so that perhaps she would be perceived as less of a threat. At first the tactic seemed to work. The creature stopped backing up and stared at her. It cocked its head sideways, studying her.

Then without warning it opened its mouth wide and let out a long, high pitched wail. The shriek was loud enough to almost be painful. Echoes of the cry rebounded from the walls. If anything else was living nearby it would surely have heard the noise.

Clattering sounded from Sam's left and right. It was time to get the hell out of there. She snatched the torch back up from the floor again and ran deeper into the room. Fleeing back the way she had come seemed like a bad option. The things could just follow her, eventually trapping her against the collapsed entrance. The last thing she needed was to have them camp out on top of her bind point.

Instead she raced deeper into the room. There was a well in the middle of the open space, set midway between the columns. On the far side of the room rose a short flight of steps, with what had once been a pair of heavy doors set into the wall at the top of the stairs. The doors were ripped open now. One lay flat on the ground, while the other was askew and hanging by a single hinge.

That seemed like her best bet for escape. Sam made for the broken doors, but as she reached the bottom step more of the scaled things scurried out from the space beyond the broken doors. She backed away in a hurry. There were six of the them coming down the steps toward her. The one she had fought seemed weak, but six at the same time seemed a little much, especially in her weakened state.

Health 25/30, Stamina 93/100, Mana 50/50.

She kept backing away, looking for a way to gain some sort of advantage over the creatures. The sound of more scurrying from behind her made her glance back. Her little friend from earlier had recovered his dagger, and now he advanced on her rear. He'd picked up more friends, too. Another four of the creatures closed alongside him.

Eleven of the things? She was surrounded, with no way out. If she could win through the batch ahead, maybe she could get past the doors and lose herself somewhere beyond, although she had a sinking feeling that all she was going to discover was a warren full of these things.

She stepped forward to meet the band of six, and they rushed her. She blocked a dagger with her shield and lashed out with her sword, taking one of the things in the shoulder. Two more lashed in with their little knives though, slicing at her legs. They stood only about waist high on her, which made fighting them difficult. Her only armor was on her torso, but they ignored that target entirely and sliced at her more exposed calves and thighs instead.

Her sword cut another of them down. She blocked more dagger blows and took another nick to her leg. Sam could feel more blood trickling down her legs from the cuts she'd taken. This wasn't getting her anywhere. It was time to retreat.

She slashed hard, cutting down one of the creatures. It burbled and fell. Then something wrapped itself around her sword arm. She felt arms lock there, the heavy weight keeping her from swinging her sword freely. Sam looked down and found one of the things had wrapped itself around her lower arm. As she watched, it opened its mouth and bit down on her skin, opening another wound.

"That's disgusting!" Sam said. She swung her shield at the thing, bashing it in the head. It released her arm. But she'd been thrown off balance by the attack. She staggered another few steps and her hips came to rest against something cold.

It was the well. They'd pushed her up against the edge

of the stone wall surrounding it. Nine of the little monsters still surrounded her, all slicing and pushing at her. They were trying to throw her in!

Another dagger got in a little nick on her right leg, and Sam found she could barely support herself on that leg anymore. Sensing the moment of weakness, the creatures pushed hard against her from that side.

Sam tumbled backward. She was falling over the edge. She dropped her sword and shield in an effort to stay up, stay above, to scrabble for some sort of hold and not fall. Everything in her being fought to slow her drop.

The fingers of her left hand caught hold of the rocky edge of the stone ring around the well. Sam glanced down, seeing nothing beneath her but inky black. There was no sign of a bottom.

Sam looked back up, reaching with the other hand to find purchase on the rocks. If she fell, she was done for. With two hands on the rocks, she started working to pull her body up higher, hoping to reach the top.

A small, scaly head appeared above her fingers. It smiled at her. It opened its mouth.

"No, please don't," Sam said.

It bit down on her hand.

The wound wasn't especially painful, feeling more like a bad spider bite than the savaging her hand actually received. But it was enough to jar her body loose from the lip of the well. Sam tumbled back into the darkness, falling into that inky black toward whatever waited for her below.

Sam saw a flash of light from below her a moment before she struck something hard, and then she didn't see anything at all for a while.

20

When she woke, it was to aches from all over her body. She scanned her status almost automatically. It had become second nature to check in and see how she was doing numerically.

Health 4/35, Stamina 62/110, Mana 55/55.

She'd barely survived the fall. If she'd been unconscious for any length of time, then she must have been at a single health point or two when she hit. The fight hadn't gone as well as she would have liked, but it could have been worse. She was still alive, at least. A little icon glowed in the corner of her vision, one she hadn't seen before. When she glanced at it, a new window appeared in her view.

Congratulations! You have reached Level 2. You have five attribute points and five skill points to allocate as you choose.

Sam's head hurt. Both metaphorically and actually. Leveling up in this world had to be a plus, right? The greater her level was, the more she would be able to do. Eventually she'd be able to fight that bastard Thorsten and beat him. That was an appealing idea. The levels would probably also help her in her ultimate goal, which was getting the hell out of this place and back where she belonged.

But why did it have to be so complex? She looked at the icon on the bottom of the display and it opened up an intricate set of windows. Those windows showed her skills — she recognized the ones she'd earned so far. It also showed a dizzying array of things called attributes. She needed to sit down and learn how to manage all of this soon. For the moment, it could wait until she was certain that there wasn't any danger lurking nearby.

The room was small and round, illuminated from some source she couldn't see. It almost looked like a soft blue light was coming from the floor. Her fall had been broken by an enormous pile of bones directly under the well opening, which was in the ceiling about fifteen feet above her. Climbing out wasn't going to be an option. She'd need to find another way.

Sam shook off bits of the bones. Some of them still had some meat clinging to them, and Sam shuddered a bit as she brushed those bits from her clothing. The mess looked like a mix of skeletal remains from a variety of animals. Some skulls looked human or vaguely human. Others were bits of rat or some other animal. The whole mess was disgusting, but had probably saved her life by breaking her fall. If she'd slammed into the hard stone floor instead of the heap of debris, those last few health points might have been forfeit. She shivered at the idea of how close she'd come to death.

Dying shouldn't bother her, not here. After all, death in this place was just an illusion. But somehow she couldn't shake the feeling that if she died here, that would be it. She'd be stuck. Escape from this virtual world would become impossible. That would be the end of the Sam that was, out there in the real world, and she'd end up trapped in this place forever.

Intellectually she knew that was just bad science. These games didn't work like that. Your consciousness was projected out into the virtual world, either from a body through a VR hookup, or by uploading a consciousness to the computer itself like most of the people who'd chosen Valhalla Online as their artificial afterlife. Death here wasn't real. It was as illusory as the clothing she wore or the sword she'd been using.

Thinking of her sword made Sam realize it was nowhere to be seen. She'd dropped everything as she started to tumble over the edge into the well. Her shield, torch, and sword had all been dropped. Had they fallen down with her? She couldn't imagine being unarmed in this place.

She rooted around in the trash, hunting for her things to no avail. All her items must have been dropped in the room above. Some little creature was probably carrying them around now. She was left with only her leather vest and an empty pouch. It wasn't much against whatever lay ahead. Digging through the pile again she found an old bone from some big animal, maybe the size of a cow or horse. It was old, brittle, and unwieldy, but it would serve as a club in an emergency.

That accomplished, she examined the room she was in more carefully. It was round, about ten feet across, and still lit evenly by that dim blue glow from the floor. Peering closely, she saw runic markings all over the stone beneath her feet. The runes themselves emitted the soft light.

Across the room from the debris pile was a low stone table, set against the wall. There was nothing else to see. No doors or windows adorned the room. The walls were smooth stone, and virtually impossible to climb. She clearly wasn't getting back out the way she'd gotten in. But perhaps the table would provide some sort of answer.

Like the floor, the table was carved all over the top and sides with blue-glowing runes. Sam had seen Norse runes before on a few occasions. These looked a lot like the ones she'd seen, but she didn't know the alphabet well enough to be certain they were the same ones. The game creators might well have styled the runes here directly after those from the real world. It seemed to match their general motif.

Sam traced the lines of runes with her fingers carefully, without actually touching them. Nothing happened. She sighed, and hoping that she was not about to activate some horrible trap, she touched the table.

A window popped up in her vision.

Kaladesh was once a center of magical learning. Home to great Dwarf artisans and makers of elder magics, many people from a variety of races once traveled to this place to study with the masters here. They brought wealth with them, which caused the fame of the hall to grow even more.

That wealth was likely what brought the darkness upon them. Evil came to the place. Some say that it was summoned by a careless wizard who resided in the hall. Others have claimed that the hall was doomed when they tunneled too deep and encountered an ancient enemy that struck them down. Whether either tale is true, or if some other thing happened, no one alive knows.

Except the people who wrote this silly script, Sam thought to herself as she read on.

You have discovered the lost magical hall of Kaladesh. The task to undo the evil here and rediscover the runes of magic which once safeguarded this place is one only the mighty should undertake. Do you accept this quest? Y/N

"Hell of a time to ask me now!" Sam complained aloud. It wasn't like she had a lot of choice at this point. There didn't seem to be any other way onward except to take the damned quest on whether she was 'mighty' or not. Out of spite she looked at the No answer anyway. The entire speech disappeared from her view.

Nothing else happened. She wasn't struck down, but she wasn't transported out of the place either. She was still stuck at the bottom of a well, in a glowing room with no way out.

"God damned programmers and their shitty ass code," Sam said, touching the table again. The same speech appeared in her vision. This time she didn't hesitate, and just looked at the 'Y' answer. It highlighted and then clicked. It wasn't like she had a lot of choice about it.

The wall to her left rumbled. The cave wall slid away, revealing a passage beyond it. Like the room she stood in, the hall was dimly lit by trails of blue runes on the floor.

"I guess we follow the trail of breadcrumbs and see where it leads," she said.

21

The corridor was only about six feet tall, arched at the top. Not a single cobweb broke up the passage. It was utterly clear, like someone had dusted the place regularly. That was creepy enough. The silence, the dim blue light, and the feeling of a mountain of stone above her head all added to the ambiance.

"Not where I'd pick for a vacation home, whether I was a dwarf or not," Sam said.

After about twenty feet the passage opened up into another circular room. This one was larger than the last. It was at least twenty feet across. Here, the floor was glowing like it had been in the first room. But the trails of runes seemed more focused here. There was an outer ring of runes which ran around the edge of the room. Then there was an inner ring which surrounded a pedestal, upon which rested a book.

Other runes traced paths between and around the two circles. Sam stared at the runes for long moments, almost thinking that they moved and twisted like a living thing when she looked out of the corner of her eye. But when she looked directly at them they remained still.

There was one exit from the room, a doorway just like the one she had come through on the far side of the room. Beyond it was another hallway just like the one she'd come in from.

She carefully stepped out onto the floor. She couldn't proceed without crossing the first circle of runes, and for some reason she was loathe to do that. Sam winced inwardly as her foot stepped down inside the first circle. She paused, waiting to see if something was going to happen, but there seemed to be no effect. Somewhat relieved, she continued further into the chamber. If the runes were just there as lighting and special effects, why the concentric rings? It was either there for a reason, or it was a red herring. But which?

Sam examined the book and the pedestal for long moments. At first she had in mind to simply pass by, continuing down the hall ahead and looking for a way out of this place. But something about the book made her hesitate. It was clearly either a trap or a treasure. Perhaps both. If it contained information that she needed to get through this place, then she might get into more trouble later for not having it.

But if it was a trap, then she should pass it by.

Sam tapped the inner ring of runes with her bone club. Nothing happened. The room didn't explode, or the ceiling start descending, or anything else crazy. She'd had visions of setting off a trap like the hero in an Indiana Jones movie, but it didn't seem like that was the case. Feeling more daring, she stuck a toe in the air over the inner ring of runes. Nothing happened.

Feeling a little foolish for worrying so much, Sam

relaxed at last. The runes were lighting, special effects to make the chamber look cool. The book was probably just more information about the quest she'd accepted. She stepped past the ring of runes onto the pedestal. Sam felt herself hold her breath despite herself, but still nothing untoward happened.

"Just lights," she said aloud. Her voice seemed to carry and echo down the hallways, and she resolved to speak more softly. She opened the book. A new window appeared in her vision.

You have found a book on Runic Magic! Because you have the Rune Binding skill, you can use this book to learn more about Rune Magic. Would you like to use the book? Y/N

Learn magic like the lightning Harald had wielded, or Thorsten's earthquake? Sam felt herself growing excited. Even if she could only gather a fraction of the power those men had, it would still be a massive boon for her. Sam stared directly at the letter Y. It glowed briefly and then the message vanished.

The book flashed with a bright blue light. Sam smelled ozone, and the air itself seemed to crackle with power. She turned to the first page of the book and read it quickly. Then she flipped the page and read the next. Soon the pages were flying beneath her fingers. She'd never read this fast before, not even when cramming for finals in college. Yet somehow she knew instinctively that all the information she was taking in would be retained.

At last it was over. The book crumbled to dust in her fingers. A new window appeared in her vision.

You have learned the rune Ken. Ken is the rune of the torch, of fire and energy, of light turning back darkness. Your understanding of this magical rune is at level I.

Continued practice will increase your level with the skill. Higher levels will result in new spells becoming available to you.

You have learned the spell fire bolt. This spell is at level 1. Continued practice will increase your level with this spell.

Sam could feel that it was true. She knew that if she positioned her fingers just so, and traced just the right pattern in the air that it would call forth a flaming arrow which would fly at whatever target she directed. On a whim she stared at a point on the wall, focused her will, and activated the spell.

Her fingers traced the necessary pattern almost of their own volition. A second later sparks appeared by her fingertips. As she continued focusing her well the sparks grew into a burning bolt about a foot long. As soon as it appeared, the bolt sprang forward as if shot from a bow. It struck the wall at the spot Sam had targeted, exploding in a burst of sparks. She stepped over to the wall, examining the scorch mark which had been left behind. The wall was undamaged, but it was still warm to the touch.

"This is way too cool," Sam said.

As if in answer to her words a chill breeze flowed across the room. Sam turned quickly, but didn't see anything. Nothing stirred. Nothing had changed in the room except for the book, which was gone now. Only dust remained. Still Sam couldn't shake the feeling that something was nearby, watching her.

"Is someone there?" Sam asked.

The voice which replied to her sounded scratchy and cold. "Did you think that power came without a price?"

That definitely sounded like a threat. Sam readied her bone club in her left hand, while preparing to cast her spell again with her right. She might not have a sword anymore, but with this new spell she was far from defenseless.

"Show yourself," Sam said.

She might have felt like she was ready, but nothing could have prepared her for what flowed out of the dark hall into the room before her. At first Sam thought that it was a person, wearing jet black robes. The cloth of its garment was so dark it seemed to eat up the light emitting from the floor. Sam remained ready to fight as the figure approached. Not every person she'd met in this world was a friend, and some had been outright dangerous, but she felt the flaring of hope in her chest. If this was another human being, perhaps they knew the way out. If she could only convince them to help her, she might get free from this prison yet.

Her hope died as soon as she saw the face hidden beneath the robe's hood. Where skin and eyes and flesh should have been, there was only bone. A bare skull leered back at her astonished face.

22

Sam had never seen anything like this, not outside of a movie. Even more than the scaled creatures upstairs, this thing stirred feelings of dread in her heart. It stepped toward her, each footfall silent except for the subtle swish of cloth against cloth. Sam stepped back from it involuntarily, stumbling against the cool stone wall behind her. It's just a game, she reminded herself. This was just a creature dreamed up from the imagination of some geek and rendered in 3D for the amusement of the people playing. Nothing more.

She believed what she was saying. Mostly, anyway.

"Young wizard, your powers are weak," it said with a voice that sounded like something crawling from a grave. "That which you have stolen is not free. You must pay the price."

"I didn't mean to steal from you," Sam said. "If you'll help me get out of here, I can get you coin." She still had a small supply of money stowed away in the game bank. But somehow Sam had the feeling a cash payment wasn't what this monster had in mind. She kept her spell ready to fire.

"The payment will be your life!" It began tracing lines in the air with bony fingers. Sam could feel magical energy building up as it worked. She wasn't going to sit around and wait for it to attack. It was time to put her spell to the test. She concentrated, calling up her own magic. Her fire bolt launched forward and struck the thing squarely in the chest. Sparks burst around the thing, singing its robes, and It staggered back. Heartened by the success, Sam fired another magical bolt at the thing.

This time her magic stopped in the air about a foot in front of the monster. It struck some sort of purple barrier floating in the air in front of the skeletal sorcerer, detonating there harmlessly.

"I told you that your powers were feeble, and useless against me," it said. "You are far too much the novice. You should never have come here."

"I didn't want to come here!" Sam shouted back.

The skeletal figure didn't seem to care. It fired a blast of force toward Sam. She dove sideways, feeling the icy burst spatter against the wall where she'd just been standing. If she'd been a second slower it would have caught her! The wall took the brunt of the magic instead. Icy tendrils ran up and down the stone surface, delving in, cracking the rock. Sam shuddered to think what it would have done to her.

She fired her bolt again, with the same result. The flame never reached her target at all, exploding in the air in front of it instead. It cackled at her and readied more magic of its own again.

But had the shield seemed just a little less bright? Was it moving just a little faster in its spell casting, trying to rush through the work to blast her again? Maybe she could get through the shield if she just hammered it enough times. Sam readied and fired her spell again, hoping she could wear the thing down. Her spell broke on the purple shield just like the others, but she could see signs that the skeleton's defense was weakening. The purple light was less bright, and it flickered as her fire bolt struck.

The skeleton returned fire, blasting her with another burst of cold. Sam flinched away but wasn't able to evade the attack entirely. The cold caught her left arm, and where the magic touched her Sam lost sensation entirely. She looked down at her arm and realized it had frozen solid. She couldn't feel it because it had been turned into a block of ice. The club tumbled from her fingers.

Sam tried to ready another burst of magic, but not even sparks came at her call. Confused, she wasn't sure what was wrong with her magic until she looked at her status bar once again.

Health 6/35, Stamina 98/110, Mana 5/55.

The mana — that had been zero when she first arrived. It had to be the source of the power for her spells. She'd used the fire bolt five times, and burned through almost all her mana pool in the process. As she watched, the number ticked back up to six mana, but it wasn't going to be enough to get off another fire bolt anytime soon.

She reached for the club, hoping to grab it from where she'd dropped it on the floor. But before she could wrap her hand around it the skeleton rushed in toward her. Bone fingers locked themselves around her throat. It hauled her upright in front of its face. Sam flinched away from the sight. She beat at the thing's grip with her uninjured arm, but it was too strong. The fingers tightened their grip.

All at once she couldn't breathe any more. She heard the blood pounding in her veins as the fingers locked ever more tightly around her neck. Skeletal claws broke her skin. Sam's vision swam as she began losing consciousness. She struggled for even the smallest bit of breath, but couldn't draw anything in past the powerful hands pinning her in place.

All thoughts about the game left her. She couldn't breathe. She was dying. This thing was killing her, and she had to fight back. She kicked, she struck it as hard as she could. She pummeled the claws holding her pinned against the wall as they tightened their grip.

Her struggles grew weaker even as she became more panicked and desperate to escape. Her vision darkened. Dizziness and nausea overtook her. Sam's body was screaming for air, but there was none to be had. Her brain was starving for blood, but the bony claws were cutting off the flow of her carotid arteries. A red haze slipped over her vision. Blackness followed immediately after.

"Now you begin the payment," the skeleton said to her.

And then she died.

23

Sam woke with a start. Her hands went to her throat, where she could still feel the bony hands clutching her. The terror, desperation, and panic were all still there. It was like her death had been a moment ago. Like it had just happened.

But she wasn't in that room anymore. The chamber where the book had been, the runic circles, and the skeletal monster were all gone. She was back near the entrance to the caves. Above her hung the four torches, the same as they had been when she first entered.

It was like none of that had happened. Except that it had. It had happened to her. Sam sank back to the floor of the cave. She lay there, wrapping her arms about herself for warmth and comfort. Her left arm was back to normal. She couldn't see the smallest sign it had been injured at all. But she couldn't get warm no matter how hard she tried.

She'd died. It didn't really matter that it was just a game. To her it felt real. She was alive again, healed and restored. But she remembered what it felt like to die, to take her last breath and not be able to take another. It was a nightmarish experience. She didn't know how these people could stand to die again, and again. This was their life. This would be her life too, if she couldn't find a way free from this place. Never really alive, but dying over and over again.

Tears leaked from her eyes. She sobbed softly. Sam cried for her loss. She cried to grieve her own death. For a long while she just lay on the cave floor, unable to move.

Even after the first pangs of hunger and thirst began, she continued to lie on the cold stones. What did it matter if she starved to death, or died of thirst? She was already dead.

That thought was enough to rouse her from her self-pity. That wasn't like her. Comfortable with the idea of dying or not, she was alive again now. Where there was life, there was hope. Perhaps even now Harald was probably out looking for her. If he found the cave his magic might be enough to free her. Then she would never need to go back into the darkness that she knew waited deep within this place.

After a while Sam felt enough better that she was able to stand and pace back and forth, taking stock of her situation. Her sword and shield had been lost during the first encounter. Her pouch and armor were left behind when she died. All that remained to her were the basic clothes that she'd worn when she first arrived in this world.

The magic had stayed as well. Sam spent some time looking at the spell, learning what she could about it. She called up one of her fire bolts and shot it at the rubble blocking the entrance to the cave. Her bolt scorched the rocks, but it didn't have enough power to move anything but the smaller bits of rubble. The larger boulders were too massive to be affected even when she unleashed every bolt that her mana could supply her with.

That did bring her to studying the status sheet in more detail. If she'd had just a little bit more mana, that fight might have gone differently. A lot more mana and could perhaps have turned the tide against the thing. She recalled that she had points she needed to distribute. While she was safe near the entrance to the cave seemed like a good time.

The ability scores were simpler than she'd first figured, now that she finally had time to sit down and absorb their impact.

Strength. Affects weapon damage. Carrying capacity is dependent on this attribute.

Constitution. Increases maximum health. Affects resistances to some types of poison and disease.

Dexterity. Affects ranged weapon accuracy and damage. Affects melee weapon accuracy. Increases stealth skills.

Intelligence. Determines spell damage and impacts magic in other ways.

Spirit. Determines base mana level. Increases mana regeneration rate.

Charisma. Impacts interactions with non-player characters (NPCs). Increases effectiveness of song based magic.

Song based magic sounded interesting. Sam hadn't seen any sign of that at all yet. But she wasn't sure where she could learn such things either. Also, to date most of her encounters with hostile 'NPCs' had been *really* hostile. She had the feeling that all the charisma in the world wasn't going to make that skeleton less likely to try to kill her, for instance. While the attribute might have an impact down the road, she trusted her own people-skills to help her manage interactions with the actual players in the world around her. For the time being she needed to get better at combat.

It seemed like there were really three tracks. She could work on physical combat — hand to hand battle with swords and axes and such. Or she could choose to push more points into dexterity and boost her ranged weapon skills. That would help her melee ability a little as well, but she'd need strength to excel with hand weapons.

The problem with both of those courses of action was that they required weapons. Right now she didn't have any. Sam didn't even have the damned bone that she'd grabbed from the pile. Even that was gone, and there was nothing around to replace it with. Her sword and shield were somewhere in the caves beneath her.

A sinking sensation in her gut said that unpleasant as death had been, she might be in for more of them before she was done with this place. The quests and monsters here were designed for experienced players. She'd stumbled into something that novices should never have gone near, and she'd plunged headlong in anyway.

If she was going to get herself out, it seemed best to not count on having equipment with her. Every death would result in her losing everything. But magic would stay with her. Her spells would always be available to her, even without her equipment. That meant a lot, in her situation. Always having a weapon, no matter what? That was everything down there.

She looked over the information a few more times before deciding where to put her points. Sam had five in each stat, and five to spend. Was she going to get five more every time she leveled? If so, it meant that levels had a huge impact on overall ability in the game. She couldn't know for certain. Hoping that she wasn't screwing up horribly, Sam elected to put three of her points into intelligence and two into spirit.

Checking her stats again, she saw that her mana had gone up immediately.

Health 35/35, Stamina 110/110, Mana 55/75.

As she watched, the mana increased to fifty-six, and then fifty-seven. It did seem like it was recovering a little faster than it had before. Since her fire bolt was costing her ten mana points each time she cast it, she could fire it seven times now before she was out of power. It wasn't much, but it was a lot better than she'd had before.

Next, she looked at her skills. She'd picked up a bunch of them during her few days in Valhalla. Mostly thanks to Harald's generosity. She had Spear and Shield, Wound Care and Running, Endurance and Sword skills, all thanks to his help. And she couldn't forget Rune Binding, which was probably the thing that had allowed her to learn the rune magic at all. She owed Harald a hell of a thank you.

Since she was counting on her magic skills to get her out of this mess, it seemed to make sense to put her points into those skills. The rune Ken was listed as its own skill, as was Fire Bolt. Both of those were obvious targets for the five bonus skill points she'd acquired when she leveled up. But when she tried to add a point to Flame Bolt, the assignment failed. A window popped up in her vision.

Fire Bolt is a sub-skill of the rune Ken. Sub-skills cannot be raised higher than the skill under which they are assigned.

That made sense. Sam brought her attention back to Ken. It was also at a skill level of one. She needed to boost it up a rank, then boost Fire Bolt. She tried to add a point, but...

Ken is a sub-skill of the Rune Binding skill. Sub-skills

cannot be raised higher than the skill under which they are assigned.

"Argh! Really?" Sam huffed. Damn coders, always making things more complicated than they had to be.

She looked at the Rune Binding skill. It was still only level one. She tried to add a point to it, hoping that it would work.

Congratulations! You have reached skill level 2 in Rune Binding.

That was more like it. Then she went down to Ken, and added a point there. Lastly, she added a single point to Fire Bolt, which reached level two as well. She looked at the spell more closely and noted that it showed an increase in damage, but also in cost. Fire Bolt would now cost her twelve mana to cast instead of ten. She was down from seven bolts to six before her mana was depleted.

That was less than optimal, but hopefully the per-shot boost in damage would be enough to make it worthwhile. As if in answer to her thoughts, Sam saw that Fire Bolt was really two spells now. She had Fire Bolt 1, and Fire Bolt 2. The old one cost ten mana and did three to eight damage. The new one cost twelve mana and did six to ten damage. That was a very significant improvement, but the knowledge that she could still cast the old version in a pinch was valuable.

She had two more points to spend, so she dropped both of them into Rune Binding. Back in the practice field her skills with weapons had gone up just by using them. If she kept practicing enough with her Fire Bolt, it would eventually go up on its own, but only if her Rune Binding skill was high enough. Since that one skill seemed to be at the root of all her magic skills, it was the one more important to increase.

At last she couldn't think of anything else to do. She was procrastinating, putting off what she knew had to come next. The odds of anyone finding her and rescuing her from this place were as slim as ever. Whether she liked it or not, she was going to have to go back down there again and face the thing that had killed her.

24

Sam stood up and brushed the dust from her pants. She had almost nothing left, but that meant she had little left to lose as well. Her armor was gone. Her sword and shield were lost. She had no belts, no pouch, and even her feet were bare. The cold stones chilled her toes.

Somewhere down below her was a monster. And it was probably just the first of many. Waiting around up top wasn't going to solve anything, though. Sam walked over to the nearest torch and gently lifted it from where it hung on the wall. It was odd, that there were four torches again. She was certain one had been lost somewhere in the halls below. Just another strange quirk about this strange place.

She held the torch in her left hand so that she could keep magic ready at her fingertips with her right. The scaled creatures that had fought her in the first room might have left their hall. Sam had the feeling they were more or less locked to their little domain, but she couldn't be certain. Caution seemed wise.

Nothing waited for her in the hall. The way was clear all the way to that first door, which had been firmly closed again. Sam tried to open it, but it was stuck fast. She sighed, and use the iron ring to knock on the door again. As soon as she had knocked, the door open slightly again.

"Nothing like a door that insists you alert your enemies when you arrive," she said. It made sense, though. Whether the visitor was coming for tea or to hit you over the head, it would be good to know when someone arrived.

Nothing was waiting for her inside the hall. No little scaled creature stood there trying to stab her with a dagger, this time. Sam heaved a sigh of relief. She kept her hold on her magic anyway, the spell ready to flash at a moment's notice.

Now that she had more time to look around, Sam could see runes similar to those she had discovered downstairs. The ones on this floor weren't glowing, but they decorated the columns. And many of the floor tiles also bore a rune. Sam spotted one such tile which bore the Ken rune, the one she had learned about from the book. She traced the ruin on the floor with her finger. Nothing happened, but it was comforting.

She approached the well, wondering how she was going to get down inside. Perhaps it would be better to explore more up here before descending? She wasn't sure, and wasn't certain how best to get to level below anyway.

Sam was still pondering her next move when she felt a sharp prick in her neck. She reached up to touch the injury and her fingers came away bloodied. Something small had stabbed her! She touched her neck again and found a tiny dart. She pulled it free and held it in front of her to examine the thing.

It was definitely a weapon. Crudely fashioned from bone, the tip was extremely sharp. Underneath her blood,

Sam could see some sort of black goo covering the needle-like point on the end of the dart.

"Oh, shit," she said.

Somewhere off to her left she swore she could hear giggling. The little bastards were out there after all. They'd just let her get in, hidden off on the sides waiting for a moment when she was distracted. Then they hit her with a dart coated in — what? Some sort of poison? What was it going to do to her?

"When I get my hands on you lot, you're going to regret being born," Sam muttered. More giggles were the only answer.

She didn't feel any different yet, but she might not have a lot of time left. Sam turned and headed back toward the door to leave. If she could go back into the hall and shut the door, maybe they wouldn't dare to follow. Then she could ride out whatever they'd dosed her with before coming back.

But she only made it about halfway to the door before a chilling numbness spread in her fingers and feet. The icy feeling moved rapidly. She managed only two more steps before she lost all sensation in her legs. Unable to control her muscles any longer, her legs collapsed beneath her and she fell face-first into the floor.

More giggles, from both sides this time. Sam wanted to flinch as little hands grabbed her and flipped over onto her back. They tied her hands and feet together — why, she didn't know, since she couldn't move them anyway. Probably just insurance to make sure she couldn't attack them when the poison wore off.

Sam couldn't tell how many of them there were. It looked like even more than she recalled. She'd been right to assume there was an entire warren of the things in this place.

There was nothing she could do to talk to them. Her voice was frozen along with most of the rest of her body. It seemed like her breathing and her heart were the only things working.

Knives flashed in the things' hands. At first the movements looked threatening, but then Sam realized they weren't talking to her at all. They were discussing prime cuts with each other. The knives bit into her flesh, taking off bits of her with each slice. Because of the poison, she couldn't feel the injuries. She couldn't feel anything at all, not even the minimized pain wounds usually left her. But she couldn't move either, could only watch as the things carved her up. She'd discovered where the pile of bones at the bottom of the well had come from. The bones were from people like her, ambushed and trapped by these little beasts.

Sam shut her eyes. She didn't want to see any more of this. Some time into the experience, she passed out from blood loss. Soon after that she died. Again.

25

Sam woke with a start, back at the top of the cave after a second death. She ran her hands over her arms, over her legs. They were smooth once more, unmarred by the brutal knives of the little monsters in the cave. She shivered and lay back down. That was two deaths in as many days. Maybe she wasn't cut out for this. Maybe she should just sit tight and hope someone would come for her.

Sooner or later somebody would come. These ruins had a purpose. Nobody coded someplace this tough — or this sadistic — without intending it to be used by the players. Lots of people had probably already been through this place. Others would likely pass through it in the future. But they'd need to clear away the rubble first, and when they did she would be free.

That might take months though, and she didn't have that long. If her body was hooked up to some sort of machine, keeping her alive while her mind was uploaded here, how long could she last? If they were feeding her intravenously, her physical body could likely hold on a long time.

If she didn't have even IV hydration, well — she'd already been in here a few days. Another day or two and she probably wouldn't have a body to return to, if that was the case.

She pulled herself up against the wall, leaning into it. It'd taken all of her courage to go back down there, and the results had been disastrous. All she had done was get herself killed again. Sam envisioned trip after trip down into the cave, dying each time in new and ever more disgusting ways.

"I'd rather just starve to death up here every few days," she said. "And now I'm talking to myself again. A sure sign I'm starting to go nuts."

Magic wasn't going to be enough, not by itself. She needed cunning, too. A hell of a lot more practice wouldn't hurt, either. If she could improve her skills then her odds would increase dramatically. But no matter how good her magic got, if she wasn't playing it smart, she wasn't going to succeed.

Ultimately, she needed to outwit not the monsters she was encountering — but rather the minds that had devised this dungeon in the first place. That was going to require all her concentration, focus, and training.

When Sam first went to West Point she hadn't been well-liked, or well accepted at first. Only about ten percent of the school had been female. All of those but her had been from well-off families, with well-connected parents. Sam was none of those things. She'd grown up in a bad neighborhood deep in South Boston. Her first run-in with the cops that she could recall was when they busted her neighbor for selling drugs, when she was six. It was something of a miracle she had eventually gone into law enforcement herself.

Even getting to West Point had been a long shot from the

start. But once she was there she found she had to earn her place all over again. She floundered and struggled, competing with young adults who were smarter, stronger, or just better equipped to deal with the school than she was.

Sam wanted to drop out about two months in. The only reason she'd stuck it out was a stubborn resistance to the idea of letting them see her stay down. It was bad enough if they saw her fall. She wasn't going to give them the satisfaction of seeing her stay flat on her face after she did.

To overcome her obstacles, Sam worked tirelessly at everything she needed to accomplish. If she had problems with math, then she was doing math problems until midnight. If there was a difficulty with marksmanship, then she would get extra practice out on the range every chance she could.

This was the same sort of thing. And she would overcome it the same way.

That day and the next became a flurry of practicing her magic. One fire bolt after another left her fingers to slam against the rocky wall keeping her penned into the cave. She depleted her mana, and then rested while recovered, only to deplete it again, firing the spell over and over.

At the end of the second day she was finally rewarded for all her efforts. Her skill with the Ken rune and fire bolt spell both increased to three. By then she was weak with hunger, though. Lack of food and water was taking a toll on her body. It rained outside that night and a small stream of water trickling down through the boulders from outside solved at least that part of her problem.

Still hungry, she went to bed. She was as ready as she was going to be. Sam knew that tomorrow she would descend and try her luck in the old dwarf Hall again.

She slept restlessly, her sleep troubled by bad dreams. It

seemed strange that people would need to sleep at all in this world. After all, it was only virtual. But Sam supposed that if you were stuck in this world forever and it was your entire existence that sleep would make it feel more natural. More real. The dreams were an especially nice touch. She could have done without the nightmares, though.

She rose after resting, hungry and still tired, but as ready as she was going to get. It was time. Sam descended again into the cave, carrying yet another of the seemingly unlimited supply of magical torches. At least it looked like she would never run out of those, no matter how many times she fell prey to the monsters down there. She wasn't planning on losing this time, though. This time it was those scaly little things that were in for a shock, and it was her turn for some payback.

When she came to the door she paused for a moment, taking time to review her plan carefully. Then Sam set the torch she was carrying on the floor, so that it would be clearly visible through the crack once the door opened. That done, she used the ring on the door to knock once more.

The knock sounded, echoing within. Sam stepped quickly back away from the door as it creaked open a couple of inches. The die had been cast. Now it was time to see if she could pull this off.

She waited what seemed like a very long time. There was no sound from inside the room. Not a whisper, not one giggle, not so much as a single scrape of something moving against stone. Still she waited patiently, just outside the line of sight of anyone or anything that might appear through the crack in the doorway.

After a long while her persistence paid off. The door creaked open another inch. And then another. A small scaly snout stuck out from the doorway, followed by a scaled hand reaching for her torch.

With a rush Sam threw all of her weight into the door, slamming it shut. The creature didn't even have time to squeal. Sam heard a crunching noise as its bones shattered under her weight combined with that of the door. Blood seeped under the doorway, and a little bit of a claw was still stuck on her side.

"One down," Sam said. "A whole bunch more to go."

Then she reached up, took the iron ring in her hand again, and knocked. The door slipped open a few inches.

26

Three more of the things fell for her ruse before the others got wise and stopped poking their nose through the crack in the door. Sam chuckled softly to herself. She was sorry that she wasn't going to be able to eliminate them all this way, but four enemies down was better than nothing. It was, as she had said before, a good start.

"Time for phase two," she said.

She picked up her torch from the floor. Then she opened the door about a foot, and threw the torch into the middle of the room. The creatures seemed to be attracted to light. If she could draw some of them out...

Two of the monsters took the bait almost at once. She waited until they were almost on top of the torch and then fired her flame bolt at one of them. Her strongest bolt was now level three and capable of dealing a lot more damage. It also used up 15 of her mana, so she could only use it five times. She needed to make every shot count!

The spell detonated near the head of her target. It squealed and was knocked back onto the ground. It did not rise again. Sam was already preparing a second spell, which she fired at the other visible target. That one went down as well.

She shut the door most of the way again, leaving it open just wide enough that she could watch the room inside. Long moments passed. Nothing inside the room moved. She's taken down six of the things. Maybe the rest had decided to run off?

Sam held her ground, waiting a little longer. She couldn't afford to screw this up. Well, she could, she thought ruefully. But she wasn't looking forward to being these creatures' dinner a second time. Once had been more than enough.

While she waited Sam's mana slowly replenished itself. She still needed to be careful about managing her spells. Sling too many around, and she would find herself without power at a bad moment. Too frugal on the other hand, and she might fall to another dart while still having power available to burn. Not for the first time she wished that she knew how to cast that purple shield spell the skeleton had used in the rune chambers below.

It wasn't enough to kill the little things. In the end, she needed to get past them, not through them. It was the chambers below that she really needed to reach. To do that she had to get through the scaled critters, but she didn't need to exterminate them all. As much as she might want to get back at them for what they'd done to her, it simply wasn't practical. There could be scores of the things, or hundreds. For all Sam knew the game was generating an infinite number of them, one after another, and she would never run out.

Ultimately all she really had to do was knock out enough of the things that they were cowed. It seemed like six might have done the trick, since no more were showing up. It was time to go for it, then. She'd make a run for the well and jump inside. Once she was below she would replenish her mana and then find the skeleton mage. It was in for a surprise when they met again.

Sam snagged the knives from two of the critters that she'd killed with the door. They were rusty and not especially sharp, but they were better weapons than nothing. Then she swung the door wide, preparing to make her mad dash across the hall.

She'd barely gone five steps where there was a booming crash from the far side of the room. Sam looked, and spotted the largest version of the little creatures she'd seen so far. It was about as tall as she was, and much more heavily muscled. Even better, it was armed with her old sword and shield.

On the plus side, that meant she might be able to recover her gear after all. On the down side, it looked like the thing knew how to use her sword better than she did. This wasn't going to be the easy fight that the lesser monsters had been.

"GRARG!" the thing bellowed, lumbering across the hall with huge strides. Sam took a step back to keep some distance between them. The last thing she wanted was to close to sword range with this thing. It had to be some sort of champion for this tribe of beasties. Apparently she'd killed enough of them for the rest to decide to send their very best.

Sam traced a runic sigil in the air. A fire bolt launched from her hand, taking the thing in the top of the torso. It detonated with a bright flash and staggered the thing, but it kept coming. She fired again, but it blocked this time, taking the shot on its shield. Her shield, Sam corrected herself, watching in dismay as the wood blew apart from the spell's burst. She'd been hoping to get that back.

"Die!" it hollered at her.

Sam was so shocked at it speaking an intelligible word that she almost failed to duck out of the way of the sword coming at her head. She rolled to the right, her hand already preparing another burst of magic. Still rising from the floor when she fired, this shot went a little low. It blasted the creature's legs out from beneath it, sending it tumbling to the ground.

Sam checked her mana. There wasn't enough yet for another level three bolt. She could fire a level two spell, or wait. There wasn't enough time to think the decision through. The thing was on the ground, but it would be back up in a few seconds. She blasted it with the strongest bolt she had enough mana for. It exploded across the creature's chest, and it screamed.

"Time to end this," Sam said. Any moment now one of this thing's friends might come at her back with another of those darts. She dashed in toward the downed humanoid and slashed out with one of the knives she'd captures. A quick cut across the neck, and it was done.

Sam picked up the fallen creature's sword. Her sword. It felt good to have it back in her hand again.

"Is that the best you've got?" she called out, brandishing her weapon.

There was a small squeaking sound from ahead, near the far doors. Sam looked and saw what had to be the smallest and shabbiest of the little creatures that she'd seen. It looked unarmed, and had no armor, wearing just a little rag that covered its belly and groin. Sam couldn't tell if the thing was male or female, or if these things even had genders. But whatever the thing was, it didn't look particularly dangerous. If anything, it looked terrified. She aimed her sword at the thing as it approached, and it stopped dead in its tracks. It was quaking, staring at its big feet while it shivered. Definitely scared, not scary.

"What do you want?" she asked it. "I know you things can talk now."

"I is sacrifice," it said.

"For what?"

"For you, Great One. You have killed the Big One. The others kicked me out to be sacrifice to appease you so you don't kill them too," it said.

27

Sam stared at the creature, bemused. She didn't lower her guard, keeping a careful watch for any of the other ones which might be lurking nearby. One dart had taken her down last time. She wouldn't put it past them to try dropping her with the same technique again, using this one as a distraction.

But it seemed sincere enough. Its fear seemed to be real, especially. She couldn't help but feel a little sorry for it, even if it was just pixels and bits of data. This whole world was confusing her in so many ways. Harald, as much as he had once been human, was just pixels and bits of data himself. If her body wasn't out there waiting for her in the real world, that might be all that remained of her too.

Did that mean she ought to have more sympathy for the creature prostrate on the floor in front of her? Or less for herself? She wasn't sure, and philosophy wasn't her strong suit.

"Get up," Sam said. "What's your name?"

The creature made a sound like a llama trying to hack

up a hairball. Sam tried to voice the noise herself, gagged in the first attempt, and gave up.

"Fine. I'll call you Gurgle," she said.

"Gur...gle?" it asked.

"Yup. Gurgle it is."

"You no kill Gurgle?" it asked. Sam saw hope flicker in its eyes for the first time since she'd met the little thing. Maybe it figured she wasn't going to kill something she'd just named.

"Not unless you make me mad," she replied, raising her sword again. It shrank away, making her feel a little like a bully. She lowered the blade. "What are you, anyway?"

"Gurgle is kobold," he replied. Sam had decided it was a he. She was pretty sure, anyway, and would operate under that principle until she learned otherwise. She didn't want to give the critter the wrong idea by asking.

"Kobold?" she said. She'd heard of the things before, somewhere. Back in the real world, she'd heard about them from some game or movie or book. Apparently they were in this world as well. He nodded at her.

"Can you lead me out of here?" she asked. "The way behind me is blocked. Is there another way out?"

Hell, it was worth at least asking. Maybe it wouldn't know any other way. But maybe it would, and the kobolds might be just as happy to be rid of her after she'd killed so many of the darned things.

Gurgle bobbed his head up and down, and Sam's heart lifted. Then the kobold froze, frowned thoughtfully, and shook his head.

"Which is it?" she asked, frustrated. "Yes or no?"

"Yes, Gurgle knows a way out," he replied. "No, Gurgle cannot take you. Very bad things that way."

"Which way?" she asked. Sam had a feeling she already

knew what the kobold was going to say. She wasn't shocked when he pointed at the well.

"Of course it is. The way out has to be past the big nasty spell casting skeleton," she murmured.

"Great One has met the specters?" Gurgle asked.

"Yeah," she replied, rubbing her neck. "I've got a bone to pick with one, too."

"Gurgle can lead you," he said. He sounded dubious though, and Sam didn't have the heart to make the critter follow her down into what was certainly going to be a tough fight. Maybe an impossible fight. If she died, she would just respawn, but Sam didn't think that would be the case for Gurgle.

"That's all right, Gurgle. Go back to your people. Just tell them to stay out of my way, and that way none of them will get hurt," Sam said.

The kobold crouched down again, making pitiful whimpering noises. Sam groaned, wondering what she'd done to set him off this time. It wasn't nice having Gurgle be this afraid of her. It made her feel bad, reminding her of times when she'd been the one on the receiving end of a bully's ire. She'd handled it with a bit more spine than this. But the mirror wasn't pleasant.

She reminded herself that Gurgle might have eaten a bit of her a couple of days ago, which did make her feel a little bit better about scaring him so badly. But not a lot.

"Get up," she said. "What's wrong? I just said you could go back to your people."

"Gurgle cannot," he said. "Am cast out. Your servant. I must complete the task you set me."

"What task?" Sam asked. "Oh...shit."

"Yes shit," Gurgle said, bobbing his head up and down again. "Gurgle will die. Great One will die too."

"Well, the plan is to not die. If we work together, maybe both of us can get out of this in one piece," Sam said.

Gurgle didn't seem to be buying it. Sam had a thought, and pulled out one of the knives she'd captured. The kobold didn't seem to be armed at all. Maybe he'd just left his weapons behind. Or maybe he already was something of a runt in this pack, and wasn't allowed a weapon. She flipped the knife around and offered it to Gurgle, hilt first.

He stared at the weapon for a long moment, looking as if he thought it might bite him. "Great One asks for armed service?"

Sam wished she knew what the hell that meant. All she could do was guess here and hope that she was giving the right answers.

"Yes," she said.

The kobold took the knife and tucked it into his belt. He straightened his back, staring up at her with more steel in his gaze than Sam had seen out of him so far. All it took was a weapon to inspire that sort of change? She wished that she could do that to some people she knew back home.

"Gurgle is yours to command," he said.

"Good. What does that mean, precisely — armed service?"

"Kobolds will accept armed service for anyone who grants them weapons to bear that are greater than what they possess. The service will last for a fortnight per weapon or armor given," Gurgle said. "You have bought Gurgle's service for one fortnight, Great One."

Mercenaries? An entire race of mercenaries? She could see some interesting possibilities stemming from that. But it wasn't especially useful right now. Sam didn't have any other weapons except the knife and her sword. She wasn't giving up the sword, and the knife was only a valid gift because

Gurgle was unarmed. None of the stronger kobolds would take that offering.

Sam would have loved to lead a little band of the things down into tall, dark, and bony's domain, but Gurgle would have to do. She walked to the edge of the well and looked down. Somewhere in the chambers at the bottom of the pit was the other adversary she still had to face. Sam had hopes of finding more magic down there as well. With a few more runes and spells under her belt, she would be much better equipped to tackle whatever came her way.

28

Gurgle proved his worth right away. There was a way down the well that didn't involve leaping down and hoping you didn't break anything. Sam would never have found the little trail of carefully concealed handholds without his guidance. They were small slices cut into the rock, cunningly set so that they were almost invisible, yet they looked like each had been hollowed out with crude tools.

"Did your people carve these?" Sam asked.

"Yes," Gurgle replied. "Kobolds are good with tools, good with tunneling, good with cutting through the deep earth."

Maybe not as skilled at creating pretty work as the dwarfs had been, judging by what Sam could tell from comparing their work to that of the previous tenants. But it was impressive nonetheless. She could have hacked out handholds with a pickaxe herself, but she would never have hidden them so well.

"We hide the grips so that the specters cannot get up to us," Gurgle explained in a soft voice.

"Why make them at all?" Sam asked.

"Because sometimes kobolds lose something down hole," Gurgle explained, as if it were obvious. "Make holds to go down and get."

It seemed to Sam that it would make more sense to be careful what you dropped down the hole, but she wasn't complaining. The subtle path got them both safely to the floor. That was when she realized what Gurgle had just said.

"Wait — you said specters. More than one?" Sam asked.

"Yes. There are many. More than one hand." Gurgle held up a hand with five fingers splayed out. "Less than two hands. Gurgle thinks."

"You think," Sam repeated. Well, that wasn't the best news she'd had all day. But at least her mana was back up to full strength, and this time she had her sword as well. She had a few surprises for these rejects from a Skeletor convention.

The room was precisely as she'd left it before. Nothing had changed. Even the doorway which had opened for her when she began the quest was still ajar, the portal yawning into the blue-lit path beyond. And somewhere out there was the specter. Oh, and his half dozen or so best buddies.

Sam rechecked her stats, and got a surprise.

Health 40/40, Stamina 120/120, Mana 85/85.

Her stats had increased. All of them had gone up. She looked, and was pleased to note the little icon in the bottom corner of her vision saying that she had again leveled up. Between the efforts with her practice over the past couple of days, plus the battle with the kobolds, she'd apparently gained enough experience to reach level three. Once again, the display informed her that she had five stat points and five skill points to allocate.

Sam wasted no time allocating the points. Every single edge might count in the fight ahead. She tossed two points into Intelligence again, which gave her a nice boost to the damage of her spell. The other three she tossed into Spirit. The extra mana might be the only thing that saved her against the specters.

Her new stats display was even better.

Health 40/40, Stamina 120/120, Mana 88/115.

The mana had gone up another thirty points just by allocating the three points to spirit! True, the stat didn't do much for her beyond boosting her mana and the speed with which it recovered. But for someone using Rune Binding as much as she was, that meant a lot.

The skill points went into her magic skills again. There was no point in putting them elsewhere, really. She could prop up her sword skill a little, but Sam already knew her swordsmanship wasn't going to be what won or lost this fight. It was her magic that would win the day — or fail her when she needed it most.

"I'm ready," she told her small companion. She looked him over. He seemed almost as nervous as when he'd thought she was going to kill him upstairs. "Are you sure you're up for this?"

"Am in armed service," Gurgle replied, setting his shoulders. "The Great One commands. Gurgle obeys."

"OK, but if you're coming with me the 'Great One' stuff has got to stop. I'm Sam," she said.

"Great One Sam," Gurgle replied.

She stifled a laugh. It *was* funny, but she didn't want him to think that she was laughing at him. "Just Sam."

"Whatever Great One Sam says," Gurgle replied, rolling his eyes.

She let it go, figuring it was something she could work on with him later, assuming there was a later. Gurgle stayed a bit behind Sam as they wended their way down the passage into the chamber where the book had been. It was still there — or rather, the dust it had left when it crumbled away was still there. Sam didn't want to look for her body. It would be too creepy to see her own corpse laying there on the floor. But she was in luck, as it had already vanished. Her gear remained behind precisely where she had fallen, and she hurried over to put her things back on.

The armor hadn't helped much against the specter, but it couldn't hurt to have it on. The boots were even better. Sam was tired of having cold feet all the time, and while her toes didn't hurt as much in Valhalla when she stubbed them, it still stung.

Gurgle was watching down the passage ahead the entire time. Every once in a while he glanced back over his shoulder with longing in the direction they'd come from, but he remained alert and ready for trouble. He certainly seemed to take his duties seriously, and Sam appreciated that. She'd been lucky when she handed him the weapon. It was a whim, but it had bought her a scout and guide who'd already proven himself useful.

There was nothing else of value remaining in the room, and no sign of the specters. Sam continued into the next passage, which cut off to the right at an angle, curving like it was following the edge of a circle. She wondered at that, remembering the circles of runes on the floor of the room she'd just left. Similar runes traced along the passages. Did they just form another circle? If so, what was in their center? She had a feeling the answer lay ahead.

The whisper of cloth against stone came from behind them, warning Sam of danger just in time. She didn't hesitate. Sam knew that sound. She'd heard it over and again in her nightmares while she slept. She dove sideways, catching up Gurgle as she rolled to get the curve of the corridor between them and what she knew lay behind.

A blast of frigid air shot past her head as she ducked away. It struck the wall, freezing a patch the size of her head and spreading tendrils of frost up and down, cracking the stonework in a way that was frighteningly familiar.

"Back so soon, apprentice? Another taste of death, you want?" the specter said. Motes of amethyst and sapphire magic swirled around the thing as it readied more spells. "I can oblige."

Somehow it had gotten behind them. A secret door, a hidden path, or a magical spell — Sam didn't know, and it didn't matter. The thing was almost on top of them now, and they had nowhere to run.

29

Sam rose from the ground. Gurgle vanished, darting away from her as quickly as his legs could carry him. She didn't see where he had gone. There wasn't time to look after him. Sam was busy seeing to her own defense.

"The best defense is sometimes a good offense," she said.

A blazing bolt of flame lashed out from her hand toward the specter. It detonated shy of him, as she'd expected. The purple barrier was already in place. But the concussion from the bolt exploding drove the specter back a foot anyway. She readied a second bolt, planning to hammer her way through his defenses.

Her second shot was away before the specter could use its cold beam again. The bolt hammered away at its shield. All her practice had done its job. Sam's spells were much more effective this time. The specter's shield was beginning to come apart after only two shots.

"My turn," the specter hissed. Its spell lashed out, blasting at Sam's head. She dropped straight to a prone position on the floor, falling with bruising speed. The evasion worked, and the spell splashed against the wall behind her, but her movement fouled the preparation for her own spell. She started again, readying another bolt while rising back to her knees. At the same time, Sam drew her sword with her left hand. She wasn't a lefty, but she'd never tried shooting fire bolts with her left hand and didn't know if it would work at all. This wasn't the time to experiment.

Her third bolt flashed from her hand, blasting the shield to bits and staggering the specter. Hope rose in Sam's chest. She let loose with another bolt that blasted the skeleton back against the wall. Its black robes caught fire on its chest where the bolt had exploded. It stood back up again, and Sam wondered how much damage it was going to take before it went down. She blasted it again, and then again. The next bolt hit, scorching bone and tearing a grinding sound from the specter's mouth. But the bolt after that hit another shield.

Six bolts gone. Sam did the mental math. She had only enough for one more shot, and that shield would soak two. Her mana was coming back, but she needed a way to stall for some time. She fired the last bolt that she had power for, and it again spattered against the specter's protective barrier.

Then she ran, putting some of the corridor's curve between her and her adversary. Sam called up her stats bar, watching the mana slowly rise. She had twelve. Then fifteen — just enough to cast the flame bolt that would drop its shield. But she needed to cast two bolts, not one. And she needed to fire them both fast enough that the specter would be unable to recast its shield in the intervening time.

Sam kept moving. The specter was behind her, just around the curve of the hallway. Its cackles chased her as she ran. Sam was at twenty mana, then twenty-one.

All at once she was out of running space. The hall ended with a heavy door. Sam couldn't see a handle, lock, knocker, or anything else that looked like a way to open the thing. With enough time, maybe she could figure it out. But she was out of time. The specter came around the corner, hands blazing with blue and purple light. Its magic was building to a crescendo. Sam had nowhere to go. The next blast would send her back to her bind point and she'd be forced to start this whole thing over again.

She wanted to scream in frustration. Instead she readied her spell. At least she would go down fighting.

All at once a greenish blur leaped onto the specter's back from behind. Small hands grabbed hold of the undead thing tightly, and a tiny bright blade flashed downward again and again. It was Gurgle! His tiny blade was doing very little against the specter's bones, but the sudden attack had been distraction enough to mess up its spell. The blue light from the building spell winked out.

Sam checked her status bar again. Twenty-five, twenty-six... It was close enough. Had to be close enough.

"Gurgle, jump!" Sam shouted. She didn't delay any more than that. She fired her spell. The flame bolt darted from her fingertips and slammed into the specter's purple shield. Sparks flew, and the shield shattered. Sam was already preparing the next spell. She just needed one more mana... And there it was! She had fifteen again, and fired.

The specter hadn't time to recast the shield spell. The last fire bolt slammed home, exploding in the skeleton's face. It shrieked, an unearthly sound. The blast sent it reeling backwards several feet. It smacked against the far wall of the corridor with a bone-crunching sound. Sparks from the spell set corners of the robe alight, and the specter batted at the small flames, trying to put them out.

"Oh no, you don't," Sam said. It was time to finish this. She might not have any mana left, but she had her sword. She drew the weapon with a hissing sound and closed the gap as quickly as she could. The smell of scorched bone and burnt wool mixed in the air, and she wrinkled her nose. Sam sent her blade through a hissing arc, hoping to take the specter's head off with one shot.

It blocked, one forearm shattering when her sword smashed into it. The specter screamed again, the sound like nails on a chalkboard to Sam's ears. She gritted her teeth together and ignored the sound as best she could. She raised the blade and smashed it down toward a skeletal shoulder. The thing blocked with its other arm. Her blow shattered that one as well.

"Impossible! I cannot be bested by such a novice!" the specter cried out. "Curse you! But my brothers will hear my death. They will come for you."

"Cliché bad guy is cliché," Sam replied. Couldn't the programmer have come up with a better line than that?

Sam was tired, worn to the bone, exhausted from the spells and the running and the battle. She put everything she could into one more sword swing. Her blade whistled through the specter's neck vertebrae, shattering the bones. Its head flew clear, bouncing off the wall before settling to the ground. The brilliant blue lights in the thing's eyes went slowly out. There might be more specters coming after her soon, but for now this battle was done.

"Let them come," Sam said.

30

Sam slumped against the wall. It had been a long time since she'd felt so completely wiped out. Sheathing her blade, she looked around for Gurgle. If he hadn't managed to get clear before her blasts hit, he might have been badly hurt. In the heat of the battle she hadn't been able to make sure that he'd been safely away.

It occurred to her that it was a little strange to be worried about the kobold, especially after its fellows had sliced her up into bite-sized chunks the other day. But Sam had to admit that she hadn't seen Gurgle there. None of the kobolds who'd captured her had been as small as he.

"Is safe now?" Gurgle's voice whispered. The sound came from so close to her ear that Sam jumped, almost drawing her sword again.

Gurgle was about halfway up the wall, clinging to tiny handholds on the rock wall. His reptilian face was difficult to read, but Sam could see some fear remaining in his eyes. Probably of the specter, but also maybe of her. She realized that her hand was still on the hilt of her weapon and relaxed her grip.

"Is safe," she replied, giving the little creature a smile. "In no small part thanks to you. Well done."

"Is true?" Gurgle asked.

"True," she replied. "Your timing was impeccable."

Sam found her smile coming a little more easily. It really was true, too. The specter had been about to blast her. If the kobold hadn't struck at precisely the right moment she would have lost the fight.

Which reminded her that she wanted to make sure the specter was absolutely no longer a threat. She was pretty sure the thing was dead, but it shouldn't have been alive in the first place either. Sam glanced over at the thing's body and was surprised to see the skull had already crumbled to ashes. The body seemed to be doing the same, and the robes were gradually sinking and falling as the body beneath them continued its accelerated rush into dust. It looked like time was catching up with the undead monster with a vengeance.

Sam toed the robes, wondering if it was worth trying to salvage them. She didn't think she could ever wear the stuff without thinking about the horribly creepy monster that been the previous owner. She was going to have enough nightmares about that thing's claws around her throat without wearing its clothes. As she shifted the cloth with her toe, Sam heard something clink against the floor.

She tried to recall if the specter had been wearing anything that would clink like that. Going down on her hands and knees, Sam searched what was left of the body, finally finding a small amethyst pendant on a leather thong. There was a rune carved into the jewel. As Sam picked it up, a small window popped up into her vision.

You have found magic jewel of Rune Magic! Because you have the Rune Binding skill, you can use this jewel to

learn more about Rune Magic. Would you like to use the jewel? Y/N

Well, that was for certain a yes! This jewel was just like the book she'd found, another way to collect additional rune magic skills and spells. Did all the specters have these things? The quest she was on said something about collecting the runic lore of the dwarf hall. Maybe there were more to be found than just these two. She clicked yes. Every bit of magic she could add to her arsenal would help. The amethyst crumbled to dust the same way the book had.

You have learned the rune Algiz. This is the rune of the shield, of protection from one's foes. Your understanding of this magical rune is at level 1. Continued practice will increase your level with the skill. Higher levels will result in new spells becoming available to you.

You have learned the spell Shield. This spell is at level 1. Continued practice will increase your level with this spell.

Sam glanced over the stats for the spell. It lasted for up to five minutes per level of the spell, and soaked up a bunch of damage from spells or ranged weapon attacks, but it wouldn't help against things like a sword or axe. The spell cost twenty mana to cast at level one, though! That was a ton, and she wondered how often she could even use something like that.

Still, it was useful to know that the specter had never really had protection against her sword. That bit of information might come in handy.

The immediate threat was clearly over. This specter wasn't coming back anytime soon. She was better armed against the next ones she'd meet, too. It was time to look into how she could press on. They were blocked from progressing any further into these chambers by that damned door she'd run into. She walked back over to the door to examine it.

It was made of wood, bound at the hinged side with copper fittings. Sam ran her fingers over the wood, which was smooth to the touch like only very old boards could be. She could almost feel the weight of all the other fingers which must have touched those planks to wear them into such a velvety texture. Along the outer edge of the wood were traced a variety of the same sort of runes that she'd seen everywhere else in this place.

It lacked a handle, but it didn't open when she pushed on it either. There was no knocker, no ring set into the wood. Nothing at all that gave a clue about how it should be opened.

"Any idea how to open it?" she asked aloud.

Gurgle walked over to the door, rapped it with his knuckles softly. He placed his ear against the wood. Then he scrambled up the hinged side, tapping and touching each hinge in turn, one after another. Sam watched the entire process with fascination, wondering at the elaborate system the small creature had devised for opening doors. Finally Gurgle hopped down from the door and looked back up at her.

"Well?" Sam asked.

"Gurgle has no idea," he said. The little kobold gave a slow, sad shake of his head. "No idea at all."

"Then what were you..." Sam started to ask what all the show was for, but gave up. "OK, then. Maybe I can blast our way in. Stand back."

Gurgle backed up, and Sam traced the rune in the air to invoke her fire bolt. She was about to launch it through the air, hoping that it might smash through the wood. Before she could pour mana into the spell, she heard a click from the door.

Sam froze. Had she set off a trap? She stopped her casting. A moment later the door clicked again, but there was no other noise. She held her place for a few more minutes, but there were no other sounds, and no sign she'd set off anything.

"What's that about then?" she asked.

She slowly traced the rune in the air again. The click came the moment she finished tracing Ken in the air. It was sensing the rune. On a hunch, Sam walked up to the door, placed her hand against it, and pushed.

The door which hadn't budged at all before swung open easily now, allowing her passage into the hall beyond. Sam beckoned to Gurgle, and they went through together.

31

The room was about fifteen feet across, round, and lit with the same blue light radiating from the floor as the other rooms and halls in this place. Two doors led from the room. One was on the right, the other to the left. Sam figured that the one to the right would be toward the center of the circular path she'd been taking. The one to the left would lead outward.

Her pulse quickened when she saw what else the room contained. Another pedestal was set into the middle of the room. On top of the pedestal was another book, just like the first one Sam had gotten her initial spell from. More magic! She couldn't wait to get to the book. Quick steps took her toward the center of the room.

But she'd only gone a few feet before something clicked under her foot. She looked down and saw a baseball sized rock sink into the floor. She'd set off some sort of trigger. There was a grinding noise and she spun toward the sound. The door was sliding shut again! Sam had the feeling it wasn't going to be so easy to open this time.

"Stop it!" she called to Gurgle.

The kobold turned, but the door was shutting too swiftly. It ground closed before he could so much as get his fingers into the gap. There was another loud click as the door locked itself.

Shaking her head, Sam continued to the pedestal. She opened the book, hoping to at least get something out of this mess, but the tome was blank. The entire room was just a trap for the unwary. Sam cursed under her breath. She'd taken the bait, fallen right into the trap.

"I think we're about to have company," Sam said. "Stay alert."

Gurgle nodded nervously but didn't reply. He pulled out his knife and held it up without looking all that dangerous. Sam knew that appearances could be deceiving, though. He'd helped her before. She hoped that he might prove useful again.

Sam decided to cast the Shield spell so she'd be prepared when the other shoe dropped. The spell would hold out for several minutes, and that was time her mana could be restoring itself. She'd need every point if another specter came through one of those doors.

She'd never cast this spell before, and was still curious about how this all worked. As soon as she triggered the spell her left hand reached out into the air in front of her. It felt like this was some muscle memory activity that she'd done a thousand times before, even though it was her first time casting the spell.

Sam reached out with her left hand, tracing runes in the air. A purple energy flowed out around her hand, and then extended itself into a shield. The shield faded from her view, but there was a tiny purple icon at the bottom of her vision telling her that it was still active.

The timing was excellent. No sooner had she cast the

spell than the doors opened. Both of them — the door to her right and the one to her left — opened at the same time. Blasts of magic burst through both doorways, blue light slashing through the air toward her. The attack came out of nowhere. Sam didn't have time to dodge out of the way, and the blasts splashed over her shield.

Her magic collapsed under the combined onslaught, but it held long enough for her to dive to the floor. Some of the cold leeched through, burning her shoulder where it touched her as she dropped. Sam rolled, every rotation sending flashes of pain through the injured shoulder.

Health 31/40, Stamina 114/120, Mana 97/115.

She came to her feet and recast her shield. There wasn't any choice; she would never survive those blasts without it. Her mana dropped another twenty points. This fight wasn't going to be won with fire bolts, not with her mana being burnt on shields so rapidly. Another blast of ice magic hit the pedestal from both sides, but the room was wide enough that it impacted far from her.

Were there two specters attacking? She'd barely managed to kill one of them, last time! Two at once would be damn hard, and her mana was already down a bit. She drew her sword and held her position. If she went after one of the things, her back would be turned to the other and she'd be cut down by their magic. Better to make them come to her.

Sam didn't have long to wait. The specters stepped into their respective doorways, one from each of the open doors. Each looked identical to the one she had fought before. They wore the same black robe that revealed only their skeletal face and hands. Their steps were slow, even graceful, their long black robes making them look almost like they were floating instead of walking. They looked for all the world like some artist's cartoon rendering of death.

Except this was no cartoon. These things could hurt her. They could kill her. And while she would come back to fight another day, she'd already faced that unpleasant experience twice. She was about done with it.

"You have stolen magics that are not for you," the specter on the right said. "You must pay the price."

"I'm short on cash right now," Sam quipped. "Can you take an IOU?"

Their response was to raise their hands in unison, blue light gathering around the finger bones as they prepared another spell against her. Sam didn't give them time to get the shot off. With a yell, she rushed the one on the left. Her sword flashed through the air, slicing the thing's casting hand clean off. It staggered back away from her blow.

The other one wasn't standing around while she attacked, though. A burst of magic slammed into her shield from behind. Sam saw brilliant flashes as the violet energy of her spell warred with the blue ice magic in the corner of her peripheral vision.

"Shield spell doesn't help so much against swords, does it?" she said. Her blade sliced at the specter again. It raised the injured arm to block, and bits of bone flew from it. Sam hacked again and again, hoping to take it down before the other specter could blast through her shield spell. The specter's robes fouled her strikes a little, but each blow still shattered bones, breaking the monster apart a little at a time.

The other opponent was taking a long time to fire off its next spell, come to think of it. Sam was about to turn and see what it was up to when bony fingers closed on her shoulders from behind. An ice-like chill spread through her body from the contact. Her legs lost their strength and she sank to her knees. The sword clattered from freezing fingers too numb to hold on to the hilt any longer.

"The shield is indeed weak against physical attacks," the specter behind her whispered into her ear.

The icy numbness spread, a cold so deep that Sam knew there was no escaping it.

32

Sam's breath plumed as mist when she exhaled. It was getting difficult to think. The specter's touch was so cold that it was literally freezing her to death. She tried to grab for her sword, but her fingers wouldn't close around the weapon. Sam tried to thrash against the specter's grip, but it was too strong. Its digits dug into her shoulders, breaking the skin and spreading the cold even deeper.

She screamed.

Death still felt like...dying. Her mind and body rebelled against the idea, and she fought with everything she had. There was little that she could do against the thing. It was shielded, so her magic would have almost no impact, but she summoned the fire bolt spell anyway. It might not work, but it wasn't in her to just give up.

"No hurt her!" Gurgle cried out. The grip on Sam's shoulders become one handed, and she was able to turn her head a little to see what was going on. Gurgle was dangling from the specter's arm, gripping it with all four of his limbs and trying to tear at the bones with his teeth. The specter was shaking its arm to detach the kobold. It was a distraction. But she was too frozen to make much use of it.

Sam still had hold of her magic, though. She fired the flame bolt at the only thing that might possibly save her — the floor directly beneath her.

The flame exploded from her fingers, impacting the stone. It flashed, blasting fire and sparks back up toward her. Her shield spell protected her some, but the heat still singed her skin and burned some of her hair. In the corner of her eye she could see the update as her health plummeted a few more points from the near hit. Her whole body hurt from the combination of the cold and the quick thaw her spell accomplished.

But she was warm again, damn it. Her fingers could move freely. She reached out and took her sword in a firm grip and whirled back to her feet, already swinging the weapon as she turned.

The specter had finally freed itself of the kobold. Sam saw the hapless little creature sail through the air and crash against a wall before sinking to the floor. The monster probably still had a shield in place, and would block any magic she slung at it. But that wouldn't stop her blade.

As Sam rose to her feet she corrected the angle of the swing, bringing her sword perfectly in line with the specter's neck. It cut deep, hacking halfway through the vertebrae. The specter raised both hands to its head as the skull lolled off to one side. It stumbled, almost falling from the force of the blow.

Sam kicked it square in the chest, sending it backward. She wanted to rage against the thing, to scream at it. The specter had almost killed her. It might have killed the little creature that saved her. But ultimately, she knew that was futile. It wasn't real. It was pixels and bytes. She should as much be angry at it as she was at the rain for falling.

Which didn't mean she was going to allow it to continue to exist. Her sword sang in again. The monster blocked, but collapsed backward to the floor under her repeated blows. She swung again, and this time her blade separated its head from its body. The specter stopped moving, and the bones began to crumble into dust.

Then she turned back to the one she'd damaged before. It was crawling back into the room it had come from, no doubt planning some new trouble for her. That wasn't going to happen. It had only made it a few feet inside before she caught up with it and stabbed it through the back of its skull. The battle over, Sam sagged against her sword in relief. She hurt everywhere, arms and legs burning with the effort of keeping her upright. Her stats explained why.

Health 4/40, Stamina 38/120, Mana 62/115.

It had been an incredibly close thing. She'd won by a razor's edge, really. Another few seconds under the cold magic, or if her own spell had hurt her just a fraction more, and she'd have been toast. Sam trembled at the thought of dying again. She'd had it happen twice already. The experience was...terrible. Every time, her mind told her that she was dying for good, that she was fading away forever. Of course that wasn't really so. Would she ever really believe that, deep in her bones? Or would her mind always rebel against the void?

Tears trickled down her cheeks freely. She was spent. Emotionally as much as physically, Sam felt like she had nothing left. How many more times would she be forced to die and come back? Over and over, for year after year? How could people like Harald stand it without going mad?

It was going to take forever to win her way out of this

place. This realm alone was a task that might take years. She would have to work her way to the top ranks, which meant achieving higher levels than people who had been working at the game for years. She was stuck, trapped, and didn't even know if she was really still alive — or actually dead, and doomed to remain in Valhalla until someone had the mercy to shut down the server.

Sam looked up, trying to blink away her tears. Slowly she got back to her feet. The task might seem insurmountable, but she couldn't give up. Like it or not, this was her life now. She had to find a way through it.

Taking in the room for the first time, Sam sucked in a breath. It was an armory. Most of the stuff was sized for dwarfs, smaller in size than it would be for humans. Dozens of shields and spears were racked on the walls. Stacks of helms gleamed from the floor. On the far side of the room was a set of metal armor hanging from a wooden rack. It looked big enough that it might be workable for her. Next to the armor was a sword.

It was a proverbial mother-load of medieval goodies. She could outfit a small army with all this stuff. Not to mention boost her own survival rate quite a bit. Finding all the gear gave her an idea, but first she needed to look to a friend. She turned and left the armory to find Gurgle.

He still lay on the floor where he'd fallen. For a moment Sam wasn't sure if he was still breathing or not. Did it matter? If he was pixels, should she even grieve for him if he was gone? The whole thing was confusing to her. He was breathing, if shallowly, and he opened his eyes as soon as Sam touched his arm. Seeing her face Gurgle startled the rest of the way awake and tried to rise to his feet. He slumped back to the floor with a groan.

"Lay back and rest. You've done plenty for one day," Sam

said. She smiled down at the little creature. "You saved my bacon twice now, little guy. I'd be specter food without you."

"Am in armed service, Great One," Gurgle murmured. His eyes were squeezed tight shut, his face a caricature of a wince that made Sam want to laugh out loud. "Was Gurgle's job."

"Yeah, can you explain armed service to me a bit better? I'm still not entirely sure I understand it," Sam said.

"Kobold tradition says that if arms or armor is offered, and accepted, the one who takes the arms must remain in service to the one who offered them, for a period of at least two weeks per item. Sometimes more, for very special items," Gurgle said.

"If I gave a kobold a spear and a shield, say?"

"That kobold would follow you into battle and defend you against all enemies for two fortnights, Great One."

Sam smiled. It was maybe the first real, broad smile she'd made since getting stuck in this dwarf hole in the ground. But she'd finally figured it out. It wasn't enough to just work inside the system. Grind levels? Slowly eke out Realm Points until she had enough to reach the next plane? Then do it all over again, and again, and again? That would take forever.

Nope. She was breaking the shit out of this game.

"Gurgle, I need your help," Sam said.

"Gurgle is yours to command, Great One," he replied.

33

Getting out of the chamber proved the most difficult part of the entire operation. The door to get back out the way they'd come was wedged solidly in place. Sam broke two spears trying to open it, and eventually managed to lever it about half a foot. That was it. The door was stuck fast at that point, and there was no way she could slip out through a gap that narrow.

Gurgle could, though. He dashed off down the hall, promising to return as swiftly as he could. That left Sam alone for the first time in a bit. She was tired, but this would be a crappy time to rest. That would be all she needed — for a specter to sneak up on her while she dozed. No, she'd stay alert until she got out of this place.

She went to the piles of robes and dust which were all that remained of the dead specters, hoping to find another runic pendant, but they weren't carrying much. One of them had a pouch with some jewels. Sam slipped them into her own pouch. She could sell them later. The other had a small vial of liquid. The fluid had a blueish tinge, but Sam had no idea what it was or what it might be used for. She wasn't going to experiment with it right now. Maybe once she was out of this place she'd be able to find someone to identify it for her.

It was disappointing not to find more magic there, though. The two spells Sam had learned so far were going to have a massive impact on her success. Learning more was going to be vital. She needed to master as many runes as she could, and learn all the spells she could find.

"In the meantime, I'll take inventory, I suppose," she said, walking back into the armory.

There were fifteen spears, eight short swords, and ten axes left. Sam regretted breaking the spears now, but there wasn't really anything else she could have done. The door had to be opened. She'd make do with what was left.

Twelve helmets, twenty-eight shields, and a few pairs of leg greaves rounded out the collection. Sam wondered at the lack of torso armor. Maybe the dwarfs who had lived here each had their own body armor, and had only stored other things in a collection? Or maybe there was another room somewhere filled with chainmail shirts, just waiting to be found.

She went over to the armor stand last. The armor hung there was made of interlocking metal plates, but when she picked a piece up it felt lighter than steel. It looked like it ought to fit her fairly well. She took off her leather vest, and began putting on the armor. It snugged and cinched around her, with enough give in the straps and plates to work. In fact, it felt a little bit like the armor was refitting itself to her as she put it on. Whether that was a property of this special armor or something that would happen with any armor she tried on in this world, Sam wasn't sure. But by the time she was done cinching up the straps it fit her like a glove.

Then she went to draw the sword, so that she could take

a better look at it. As soon as she closed her fingers around the weapon's hilt a popup screen appeared in her vision.

You have found a soul-bound weapon. If you draw this weapon, you will bind it to your spirit, so that it will travel with you. Soul-bound items cannot be lost on death or stolen. Do you wish to bind this item to you? Y/N

"Do I ever!" Sam said, using her glance to activate the 'yes' answer. This would solve a hell of a lot of problems. If she was understanding this right, it meant the weapon would come with her on death. She wouldn't lose everything, not anymore.

She drew the blade. It shone with a pale silver light. The blade was longer than her arm, much longer than the one she was used to. But it was thin, which made it light in her hand.

Congratulations! You have soul-bound a Dwarf-Forged Sword of Night. While holding this sword, you will have vision in darkness similar to that of the dwarf race.

Even better. While Sam didn't see that power being of immediate value in these halls, with all their rune-light, she could definitely see how that might make a difference another time. She'd earned some new tools to help her deal with Thorsten once she was free from this place.

It was a shame that the armor wasn't soul-bound as well. Then she'd be set. No more worry about what happened if she died. She'd just re-appear with all her key equipment right there with her. That would be too damned simple, though. She looked at the stats on the sword and winced a little. It was designed for someone who was level five, which made it a little overpowered for her, but still usable. It wasn't going to last her forever, though. Eventually she was going to want to get something better to replace it.

For now, it was a godsend. She'd take it. With a shield, she was ready for battle again. All Sam needed to do was get out of this place, which was easier said than done. She stepped out of the armory room and peered across the way to the other open door. It led down a short, blue-glowing hall and ended with another door.

No way in hell. According to Gurgle, there were still a few more specters floating around in the halls. The last thing she needed was to run into more of them by going off alone. She waited for her ally to come back.

It didn't take long. The scraping noise at the door alerted her to his return as he squeezed himself through the gap. Another kobold was with him. This one was larger than Gurgle. It had a wicked dirk belted to its side, and an overbite which showed rows of sharp teeth dangling from its snout. The newcomer snuffled in her direction, its hand darting toward the weapon like a nervous tick.

It wasn't alone, either. Another kobold came into the room, and then another. Gurgle stepped off to one side, looking very small and scared next to these other kobolds. Sam swallowed hard, wondering if she had just made a horrible miscalculation.

34

More kobolds were squeezing through the gap in the door every moment. They didn't look friendly or helpful like Sam's little friend Gurgle. These newcomers had squinty eyes that assessed her carefully, and hands that never strayed too far from their weapons. Gurgle was cute, in an adorably grungy sort of way. Sam had gotten used to the little guy. These kobolds were aggressive, even mean. Every time she looked at them, she could remember the way they had hovered over her while they killed her and sliced her up for meat.

This had been a terrible idea. She shivered. They were going to do it all over again, and she was in no shape to fight this many of them. She took a step back away from the door as more of them kept coming.

Once six of them were in the room, with another sliding in through the narrow gap in the door, the biggest of them planted a booted foot in Gurgle's chest and shoved. The smaller kobold crashed to the ground with a small cry.

Fire leapt to Sam's fingers almost without her thinking about it. Her hand traced the runes in the air, and a flame bolt flashed free. It smashed into the stone floor beneath the attacker's feet, knocking him to the ground. His boots were singed and smoking. He rolled around and then pulled his feet up to his face, blowing on the boots to put out the embers burning there.

Sam laughed at the sight. She couldn't help herself. The damned things were funny. Deadly, too. But it was hysterical watching the three-foot creature rolling around blowing on his feet.

They all froze at the sound of her voice. Their hands went to their weapons but held just short of drawing them. This could go very badly in a moment if she didn't play the next words just right.

"Gurgle is in armed service to me," Sam said. "You act against me if you act against him."

The wounded kobold clambered back to his feet and squinted up at her. "You defend all who are in service to you so?"

"Provided they act with honor, yes," Sam replied.

"And you want to bring more kobolds into armed service?"

"Yes," Sam said. With a storehouse full of weapons and armor, she ought to be able to work out something with these things.

"We no need little blade like that," the big kobold spat. He patted the dirk at his side. "Have blade."

"Come with me. You lead these others, yes?" Sam said. When he nodded, she continued. "Just you then. The others can wait their turn."

She led him into the armory. Sam smiled at the look on the kobold's face when he saw what was inside. His eyes grew to the size of saucers. His mouth gaped open a few inches, drool spilling out onto the floor.

They were gross, but she could deal with that. They weren't that different from handling infantry lugs, back at the base. Show them something shiny and their minds go someplace else.

"Pick two things, in exchange for two fortnights of service," Sam said.

"Two for one fortnight!" the kobold snarled back.

Sam snorted and shook her head, glad that Gurgle had given her as many details as he had. "That's not the way your folks do armed service. Anything in that pile is an upgrade from what you have. Two items, two fortnights. Or I pass you over and offer the first pick to another kobold."

He glared up at her, eyes measuring her carefully. Sam could feel him checking over her strength, the power of the spell she had cast earlier, and the defense afforded by the new armor she wore. She had to look pretty formidable.

"You found all this," the kobold said. "I could just take it from you."

"I won it from the two specters guarding it. I don't think you could take it from me. I think you would be a fool to try. Are you a fool?" Sam asked. In the back of her mind she wondered what she was dealing with here. The basic actions of the machine characters like the specters seemed simple, but this kobold was more complex. She didn't think that there were players who were kobolds — were there? Was she dealing with another human intellect? Or was she simply speaking with a machine mind that had been crafted to approximate one?

And was there really a difference between the two anymore, if you couldn't tell between them?

"I agree to terms. I get first pick," the kobold replied.

"You're their leader. Of course you do. What's your name?" Sam asked him.

"Gnash. We support you, then you defend us like you did the puny..."

Sam narrowed her eyes the moment Gnash began speaking badly of Gurgle, and he stopped speaking a moment, shrugged, then went on.

"Like the small one you have in service already?" he finished.

"Yes. Gurgle will remain my liaison with you all, though," Sam said. Mostly because she felt like she could trust the little kobold. "I will give him orders. He passes them to you, and you will command the others. Fair?"

Gnash seemed like he wanted to object for a moment. Sam could understand why. What she proposed was very close to taking orders from Gurgle, and if she understood their culture well enough the idea of taking orders from someone weaker than yourself was simply never considered. The small were beaten on by the larger and stronger. Gurgle was given to her more as a sacrificial lamb than anything else. He'd been the most expendable.

But after a moment, Gnash nodded. He searched through the gear in the armory and found himself a wicked looking axe and a heavy, iron-banded shield. The gear being built for dwarf-sized users was an asset there, as it should all work for the kobolds.

"I serve. Two fortnights," Gnash said. "I bring the others through."

It took a while, with a great deal of jostling and shoving, before everything was settled and the kobolds were armed. Sam had tucked away a shield and short sword, which she presented to Gurgle. He wept at the gift, and pledged himself to her for two additional fortnights. Then he gave her the little knife she had first handed him — the only gift he had for her. She smiled, her own vision growing a little misty. Sam tucked the present into her belt. You never knew when a knife might come in handy.

When all was said and done, Sam found herself with three dozen heavily armed kobolds before her, all of them swearing their service to her for the next month. They filled the armory and spilled out into the next room as well, where some of them batted at each other with their newfound implements of destruction. The entire mess was like a sea of kindergarten children at play — if the kids had mouths full of sharp teeth and weapons. Sam looked at them all and hoped she could maintain control.

Now that she'd begun this, she had to create discipline. She knew how to do that, though. She'd been through it enough herself, back at West Point. Once the last weapons and armor were given, and the last kobold had pledged his or her service to Sam, she glanced around the room.

"Attention!" she shouted, her voice cracking like a whip. All movement stopped. The kobolds froze in place, some of them holding in place while they were in mid-swing of a spear or axe, showing off their new toys to each other.

"When I call that out, I expect you to stop what you are doing, you tunnel rats," Sam said, stalking through them. "Then to form up into lines, weapons and shields at your sides, ready for action. Understand?"

They hesitated.

"Do you understand?" Sam roared, channeling her best drill sergeant voice.

"Yes?" one of the kobolds squeaked.

"Yes what?" she shouted back.

"Yes, Great One!!" the kobolds replied, in a ragged unison.

"I can't hear you!" Sam shouted back. She was trying not to grin. That would ruin the entire effect. If the cadre from her Hell Week at the Point could see her now, they'd laugh their asses off. The whole lot of them would be rolling on the ground. But the program seemed to be letting this shit work on the kobolds about the same as it would on a bunch of real human recruits. She had them. She had them at 'tunnel rats'.

"YES, GREAT ONE!" they all shouted back.

"You have all pledged to serve me. I will also serve you — and defend you from those who would harm you as best I can. We will fight together. The next battle lies ahead. Prepare yourselves," she said.

Sam was damned near sure there would be more specters down the hall ahead. She'd deal with them, and then she was getting the hell out of this dungeon. She had a rematch coming up with a certain asshole by the name of Thorsten. Next time, she wasn't going to be alone when they faced off.

35

Sam proceeded down the hall through the other open door, into the unexplored section of the dwarf halls. Gurgle was at her side, and a small horde of kobolds followed behind them both. She hadn't felt so confident since entering this world. This, she could do. Sure, the kobolds were more of a mob than an organized fighting force. But they were going to make short work of whatever opposition they came across.

The corridor had a slight downward slant and curved to the right as they went along, slowly bending around until Sam was certain they had gone in a complete circle. They progressed deeper into the dwarf hall, spiraling inward toward...what? There surely had to be something at the bottom of this place. With luck, there would be a way out as well, otherwise they'd have to retrace their steps. She'd be right back where she started, at that point. No, there simply had to be another exit down there. All she needed to do was find it.

Sam continued marching forward into the cool blue halls. The downward grade became more pronounced, the inward spiral sharper. She had the growing sense that whatever they were headed toward was the center of this place.

Finally the hall ended in a steel-bound door. It looked much like the ones she'd left behind up above: more runes worked into the wood, and no obvious sign of how to open the thing. Sam traced her fingers in the air, sketching a rune like she had to open the last door, but nothing happened. She stood there a few minutes, wanting to growl at the wooden thing. There was no knob or handle to pull. It wouldn't push open. Nor did it open to a rune the way the other had. She tried knocking, like she had at the first door. Nothing.

"Great One, allow us," Gurgle said from Sam's elbow. "We open door."

"You think you can?" she asked. It hadn't occurred to her to ask the kobolds. She turned and saw that several of them were setting aside arms and armor, and bringing out small picks.

"We get in anyplace," Gnash said, grinning. He was carrying a pick of his own. Sam had no idea where they'd been storing the things. She hadn't seen them before. "Kobolds cut through stone like soft mouse belly."

"Have at it, then." She stepped aside to let them try. It was certainly worth a shot. Nothing she had done was proving effective. Had she missed something up above? Some method of triggering the door to open? Was there something she hadn't done which she should have? Maybe there was another stone set someplace, like the one which had triggered the doors to close, only this one would open the door here instead. Sam had the feeling that this door was a puzzle that she was supposed to figure out.

Instead, the kobolds were going about it like it was a Gordian knot: if you can't solve the problem, cut through it.

Or around it, as the case might be! They attempted cutting through the door at first, but the wood seemed harder than steel, and resisted their efforts. They shifted their attention instead to the stones immediately beside the door. Little picks struck at the rocks again and again, breaking bits of rock clear with small pinging sounds. Two kobolds at a time worked in unison on the spot, widening the gap slowly but steadily. When the miners tired they stepped back, immediately replaced by two other workers. Sam watched the hole they were digging open up as they went along.

They paused once there was a little opening big enough for their small hands, a space between the iron banding of the door and the wall beside it. Then they reached in with questing fingers.

"What are they doing?" Sam asked Gurgle. She leaned in close to him and kept her voice pitched low.

"Look for trigger. Thing keeping door shut. Find trigger, door open," he replied.

Whatever they were doing, it didn't seem to be working. After another minute Gnash growled at the kobolds, stepping forward and shoving them out of the way. Then he stuck his own hand into the hole, reaching around inside. He pulled it out again, shaking his head, and barked more orders.

Fresh kobolds knelt down on the floor, hammering away at the base of the door. Two more kobolds stood so they leaned against the door and the stone doorway, and then a third set of two climbed them like they were ladders and began hammering at the stone near the top of the door.

It wasn't a regular door latch, Sam realized. They'd been looking for a normal latching mechanism, about at the height where a knob would have been. There wasn't one. Instead, Gnash directed them to look for locking pins at the top and bottom. The picks struck again and again with their sharp pinging sound, the blows striking sparks from the stone.

"Anything on the other side knows we're coming for sure," Sam warned. "Have your kobolds ready to jump back if the door opens."

Gnash looked up at her and nodded. He didn't quite roll his eyes, but managed to make it clear they already knew the risk. The kobolds hammering away at the stone worked a little more quickly, if anything. The tempo of their blows increased. Small shards of stone scattered against the walls and ceiling.

Sam reached down to her sword hilt, making sure the weapon was loose enough in its scabbard to draw easily. All her stats were at maximum. She was as ready as she was going to be for whatever waited on the other side.

There was a commotion from the kobolds and a flurry of action. The two breaking into the stone atop the doorway jumped down. Gnash climbed up to replace them, and reached into the gap they had made. He sawed at something inside with a small tool.

"Dwarfs make locks, keep kobold out," he muttered as he worked. "Phfah. Kobold get in anyway. Get in anywhere."

On the floor beneath him another kobold was making similar cutting motions, slicing through whatever pin was holding the door closed on that end. Sam felt sweat break out on her brow, and her fingers grew a little slippery. Her vision seemed a little sharper as adrenaline took over. For a moment she marveled that she could still feel the effects of adrenaline — even though she didn't have a body here. Did that mean she was still connected to her body? Or was that too something that had been coded into this world?

There was a popping noise as Gnash's tool finished

cutting. He jumped to the floor, putting away the little saw that he'd been using and drawing his weapon, then lifting his shield from where he'd placed it against the wall. A moment later a second pop came from the bottom of the door. The kobolds working at the base scattered back. Armed kobolds pressed in, locking their shields together. They halted immediately in front of the door and waited.

For her. Sam realized they were waiting for her word. She stepped between them, her own shield up and ready for whatever awaited them. She cast her shield spell. If there was trouble on the other side of the door, it might come in handy.

With a hard shove against the rune-covered door, she pushed it in. It groaned at first, but then flew inward, swinging back against the wall of the room inside.

36

Entering the chamber gave Sam a sense of deja vu. It looked very much the same as the room she had left behind. The similarities were so stark that she paused in the doorway, worried about tripping a trap that would close the door and lock it behind her like the one in the last room.

The room was illuminated with the same blue light as the hall outside, radiating from the same sets of runes inscribed in long swirling rows and paths. A pedestal was set into the center of the room, with a large slab of slate set atop it. More runes were carved into the face of the rock, but Sam couldn't make out what they were. This chamber was a bit bigger than the last room, she realized. It had seemed smaller at first because of the occupants.

Three specters stood still as statues inside. One was on the far side of the pedestal from her. The other two flanked it. As soon as they saw her, they began moving slowly toward her. Their gentle, easy strides carried them swiftly across the floor.

"You quest for that which mortals should not have," one of them whispered.

"Knowledge of the runes is reserved for gods and heroes," the second intoned.

"You are neither," the third added.

"We'll see about that," Sam said. She drew her sword. The specters would have cast shields of their own by now. They'd had plenty of warning. Her spells would be useless. This battle would come down to swords, and she'd brought plenty of them along.

The specters halted five feet short of her and raised their hands in unison. Sam raised her own shield, knowing it wouldn't stop their cold spell, but hoping for whatever slim protection it might add to her spell. She wasn't sure her shield would hold out against the concentrated magic of three attacks!

Thin rays of frost spat from each specter's upraised hand. But the attacks never struck Sam. She heard cries of pain from either side of her and glanced over. The specters knew she was shielded. They weren't attacking her — they were killing the kobolds alongside her! She watched as they gathered power for another blast of magic.

"Fan out!" she cried. "Don't let them hit you with the spells!"

The kobolds scattered along the wall, stepping over the dead bodies of three of their comrades. A twelfth of her force, gone in the first seconds of the fight. Sam cursed under her breath, hating the way the numbers worked out. The kobolds engaged the two specters at the sides, thrusting spears that tangled in their robes while others darted in to hack at the bony legs with axes and swords.

The middle specter raised a finger again and pointed. Sam traced where its fire was going to land. It was firing at

Gnash. That made sense — he was the biggest kobold, and likely the greatest threat. But she couldn't let it kill him.

"Gnash, look out!" she said. But he was distracted, busy fighting the specter on the left. If he heard her, he couldn't respond. Sam did the only thing she could think might help. She stepped between the specter and its intended victim, hoping her shield spell would be enough to protect her.

The blast hit her shield, which flared in a flash of purple light around her as the magics battled one another. This specter hit harder than the ones she'd fought before. Her shield held, but only just. As the ray of frost flickered out Sam felt a chill reach her bones even through her magical defense, sapping some of her stamina away. Sam staggered back against the wall, stunned for a moment. A hand reached out to hold her arm, helping her find her balance.

She looked down and saw Gnash staring up at her, wonder in his eyes.

"You do defend kobold. Even with own life," he said. Sam wasn't really comfortable with the awe she heard in his voice and saw in his eyes. She opened her mouth to protest, but he went on before she could say anything. "The little one is right. You are Great One. You fight for us. We battle for you."

Then he turned back to the fight, shouting commands to the remaining kobolds. They formed a rank, nipping away at the specters, chopping bits of bone clear. One of the creatures tried to cast another magical attack, but Sam was ready for it this time. She cast shield around the kobold it aimed at, and the blast burst harmlessly against her shield spell. The kobold was knocked to the floor, but jumped back quickly to his feet. With a quick cry of "For the Great One!" it was back in the fray.

Sam shielded herself again as she waded back in toward

the center specter. It was using its claws to fend off six small attackers, and had opened wounds on two of them already. It was time to finish this.

Her sword sliced through the air in front of the specter, forcing it to take a step back. Gurgle darted in, slicing at its thigh with a short sword. It reached out to claw his face, but Sam stepped in to block the blow with her shield. The metal frame rang as it absorbed the force, followed by a grating sound like nails on a chalkboard as the specter's talons raked across its surface.

She sliced out again and took off the offending hand. It reached out with its other claw, trying to cut her, but two of the kobolds screamed their defiance and rushed in to pin the specter with spears. Their charge drove it back two more steps until it crashed against the pedestal. Staggered, the thing stood there as Sam closed in with it. She slashed at the specter's neck, snapping the head free from its body. The skull rolled across the floor to land at her feet, face up. She stared down at the thing, which spoke to her even as the blue lights died in its eyes.

"You fought to save those weaker than you, even at risk to yourself," it said. "Perhaps I was wrong, and you are a hero after all."

"I'm no hero," Sam said. "I just want to get out of this place."

"Heroes are made by actions," it replied. Then the light was gone, the skull just a bit of lifeless bone.

To her right and left, the kobolds had hacked down the other two specters and were smashing the bones into shards. There was little left of either of them, and the kobolds were being very thorough in their work. The battle was over. Sam looked around the room and saw that it was missing the one thing she had most hoped to find — a doorway out of the place.

"Shit," she muttered. Well, there was more than one way to get out of a hole in the ground. She supposed it was too much to hope for, that she would at least once have an easy path.

The pedestal lay before her though. She stepped up and took the tablet resting there in both hands, staring at the rune inscribed on it.

You have found magic tablet of Rune Magic! Because you have the Rune Binding skill, you can use this tablet to learn more about Rune Magic. Would you like to use the tablet? Y/N

She looked at the yes answer, and another set of words appeared in her vision.

You have learned the rune Isaz. This is the rune of the frost and cold. Your understanding of this magical rune is at level 1. Continued practice will increase your level with the skill. Higher levels will result in new spells becoming available to you.

You have learned the spell Ray of Frost. This spell is at level 1. Continued practice will increase your level with this spell.

Your practice with Rune Binding has caused your skill to improve! You are now skill level 4.

You have completed the dungeon! Congratulations; you have earned 1000 Realm Points as a reward.

It was a good start. The realm points were a great bonus, but the real gain was the magic. She had three spells, which would give her some surprises to show Thorsten when they met again. Now to get out of this place. After what she'd seen her small friends do to the door, Sam thought she had some ideas about that as well.

37

The kobolds' idea of stone working might not be as pretty as that of the dwarfs, but they were efficient little creatures. Sam was amazed with how quickly they'd set about clearing the entrance to the tunnel. They pulled rocks from the jumbled landslide, pushing them up against the corridor wall. More rocks tumbled down, and for a little while it seemed like they might run out of space to put the rocks before the hillside ran out of debris to drop, but eventually a flash of sunlight broke through a small gap in the barrier.

Her workers shied away from the light at first. Even Sam's eyes needed a few moments to adjust to the brightness after so long in the dim tunnels. But then they all returned to work. Not much longer now, and they'd be through. She'd be back out into the world. Fake and imaginary it might be, but Sam had found herself missing it anyway.

She wondered what had happened to her friends. Harald wouldn't have taken her disappearance lightly. How many days had she been stuck underground? She wasn't sure, but it had been at least a few. If Sam had died, she should have respawned somewhere. One of the forts, or the castle — she would have come back. It had been days now, but nobody had come to find her. Either they'd looked and hadn't been able to locate the entrance hidden underneath all the rubble, or something was going on out there which was keeping them too busy to look for her.

If it was the latter, it had to be something big. Sam's gut said that Thorsten was making a move. Some sort of attack or power play was going on, but what she couldn't be sure.

She hefted another boulder and hauled it away from the slowly widening hole. She'd know more soon enough.

"Gurgle, can you peek out through the hole? Carefully, now. I need to be sure there's no danger out there," she said. It ought to be big enough for the tiny kobold to slip his head out.

Gurgle nodded seriously and scampered up the pile of rock to the little gap they'd made. He squeezed his body into the space, so tight that for a moment Sam was afraid he was going to get stuck there. But no — a minute later he popped out and slid back down the pile in a clatter of small stones.

"Nothing, Great One. Just trees all around. Nothing moves," Gurgle said.

Sam nodded. She hadn't thought there would be. It wasn't like she had been a major obstacle for Thorsten's plans. She'd only managed to get him to follow her at all by taunting him until he had no choice but to hunt her down or lose face with his men. She simply wasn't that big a threat.

But that was before. Now she had a small army of kobolds at her side, and enough spells in her arsenal to give him a very bad day. Six of her little troops had died in the fight with the specters, but Gnash had carefully collected their weapons and found other kobolds to replace them and finish their term of service. She was back up to a full troop of three dozen warriors.

A short while later, the hole was big enough for Sam to crawl through herself. She pushed aside a pair of rocks, shoving her way out to the surface. It felt good to feel the cool forest breeze on her face again. Her skin was slick with sweat after the effort of moving the rocks, and then struggling through the narrow tunnel.

Sam looked back at the hole behind her, shivering. The place was full of dark memories for her. Recalling the deaths she had faced in the dwarf halls, each more horrible than the last, she shuddered despite the warmth of the afternoon sun.

She was free now, but something had been left behind in that place. This wasn't so much a game to her. Not anymore. Sam thought she might never be able to take this world as lightly as she once had. There were consequences here, after all. What one did mattered. The price for failure might not be physical pain, but there were other ways of hurting a person.

Around her the kobolds had taken up watchful positions, eyeing the forest with worried looks. They weren't used to being out in the open. Sam figured they would feel vulnerable out here in a world where danger could come from any direction. If she wanted them to retain their confidence in her, she needed to organize them quickly.

"Attention!" she shouted.

The kobolds froze for only a moment this time before falling into ragged ranks in front of her. They were getting better at this drill. There was still some way to go before they'd be as proficient as your average boot camp graduates, but the improvement was enough for now. She didn't need perfection.

Sam had been pondering her next move for a while now. She needed intelligence more than just about anything else. What had been going on while she was locked away in the dwarf halls? She needed to know. The nearest fort was Klaastaad Faste. Whether it was still held by the blue faction or someone else, she could at least begin getting the lay of the land from there.

"We're on our way to scout a castle. If it's held by the enemy, we may well attack the place. I'm going to need all of you warriors at your best," Sam told the kobolds. "Are you with me?"

They cheered. Sam blinked. It was something of a surprise how touched she felt by their cheering. These were just computer images, after all, controlled by the program. But they certainly looked and felt real enough to her. She'd fought for them down below, and now they were hers. They would have her back in the fight ahead, she was certain of it.

"I want you six to scout ahead in that direction," Sam said, pointing in the general direction of Klaastaad. "Stay close enough that you can alert us if you run into trouble. Don't engage anyone you meet. Retreat and return to me."

The six kobolds nodded and dashed off.

"The rest of you, with me. We march together."

The kobolds started into a ragged march, the formation quickly blurring into something more like a mob. Sam sighed. Turning these critters into a cohesive fighting unit might be more trouble than it was worth. But it was something she ought to be good at, so it was worth trying. She barked out orders, forming them up again as they walked. Ranks slowly came back into place, and then faltered again.

Sam groaned as two kobolds tripped over a third kobold's spear. They sprawled on the ground and came up snarling. It was going to be a long hike. They had a lot to learn in a short time if they were going to stand against Thorsten's forces.

38

The little force was almost to Klaastaad before the scouts came running back. They were out of breath when they arrived, huffing and puffing. But all six of them were there, which Sam took as a good sign. If they'd run into more serious trouble, she doubted they would all have escaped it.

"Are you being pursued?" she asked. Just to make sure. But they shook their heads. "What did you see?"

"Castle, Great One. Big place. Many humans there fighting," one kobold replied.

"Did you see what color the flags on the castle were?" Sam asked. The kobold nodded and picked up a green leaf from where it had fallen on the ground, waving it like it was a little banner.

The greens must have taken the castle. Whether it was during the fight she had left, or whether Harald and the others had held out for a while before losing the place, Sam didn't know. She recalled Harald saying that the keeps changed hands often, so for all she knew Klaastaad had passed through half a dozen hands since she'd left.

Breaking that cycle was going to be tricky. To achieve her goals, she needed to not only take a keep, but hold it for an extended period. She had another twenty-seven days of kobold support. If she could hold the keep that long, it would make a huge difference in her Realm Points. It might even be enough to throw her into the top bracket so that she could pass into the next region of the game.

But first she needed to take a fort. The guard captain you had to beat to win control was tough. Even Harald had needed massive assistance to win. Sam knew she'd come a long way, but she had no illusions about being stronger than Harald.

If the fort was already under attack though, this might be the ideal time. If they could strike at just the right moment, the walls would be undefended, the AI controlled guards weakened. Swoop in, kill the attackers and the last guards alike…

It was a possibility. A serious roll of the dice though.

"Did you see what color the attackers wore?" Sam asked the scouts.

"Your color," one of them replied, tapping her armor. Bits of her armor had changed from steel grey to blue after she'd put the stuff on. Something about the game, a feature that helped one tell friend from foe, perhaps. Sam wondered if it would color everything she wore in her faction's colors. If that was the case, she found herself envious of the black faction, and incredibly happy she hadn't landed in the greens.

The blue faction was attacking the fort. Was that Harald leading the force? Or Thorsten? Or someone else she hadn't met yet? She wasn't going to ambush Harald, even if it meant losing her immediate shot at winning a keep.

There was no way to know without going in for a look.

She'd have to see for herself, and decide once she knew who was fighting whom out there. Her pace quickened a little at the thought of running into Thorsten so soon, though. She was eager for a rematch, but at the same time scared by what he had done to her before.

"We move out," she said with a firm voice. Never let the troops see you sweat. That had to be either rule number one of commanding, or number two at worst. "We go to the fort. To battle!"

The kobolds let off a cheer and reformed their ragged line. Sam took off at a light jog and the kobolds picked up their own pace to match. The clearing wasn't far, and Sam heard the battle before she could see the walls. The fighting was still ongoing, so they still had some time left. She could feel the seconds ticking away. Once the guards fell, the keep would belong to whomever had taken it. It would spawn new guards, and new gates. She'd have the devil's own time winning it then. Time mattered.

They reached the edge of the clearing around the keep without running into trouble. Sam scanned the walls. Ladders leaned against the wall in a couple of spots, and the main gate had been smashed in by a battering ram. But there was no sign of ongoing fighting along the battlements. That meant the defenders had either fallen or retreated back to the inner keep. Most likely, the human defenders were dead, leaving only the AI guards to hold the place. It wouldn't last long.

"With me!" she shouted, and ran toward the yawning gateway. Bits of broken wood lay strewn about just inside the gate, along with the bodies of several people. Both defenders and attackers lay side by side in the carnage. The fighting had been fierce there.

More bodies lay in the courtyard and along the

ramparts. Sam didn't notice anyone that she knew. The sounds of continued fighting from the inner keep drew her attention, and she pushed onward toward the battle. The keep's front doors hung open, but Sam paused a moment before rushing through. Inside might be allies or enemies, and she wouldn't know which until they were past.

"Attention!" she shouted. The kobolds formed their ranks at her command, locking shields against one another. "Follow me!"

Then she stepped through into the gloomy room beyond.

The inner keep was still festooned with green banners. The guards hadn't fallen, not yet. Smoky torches lit the place, their flickering light casting shadows and glancing off the pools of blood on the floor. Bodies were everywhere. The green force had made their last stand in this place, and they'd fought hard. Sam saw the bodies of a dozen or more green-clad warriors strewn across the floor of the great hall. They weren't alone, either. A good number of blue fighters had gone down taking the place.

The last bits of fighting were ongoing up at the far end of the hall, near the hearth-fire. The green guard captain remained on his feet, along with two other AI guards. Surrounding them were a dozen human fighters wearing blue, all of them working to take down the guards together. Even as Sam took the scene in, one of the guards dropped. The remaining two took a step back under the renewed assault. The battle was all but over.

None of the blue force had noticed Sam or her kobolds yet. They were completely caught up in their own battle, fighting to stay alive. The guards were falling, but still deadly. The captain ran one of the blue fighters through with his sword, and bashed another in the face with his shield. Sam winced in sympathetic pain as the two warriors fell.

Then she spotted the leader of the blue force. He stood a bit behind the other fighters, taking shots with his sword when a safe opportunity rose. She could sense the magic he was drawing up, preparing into a spell. It was Thorsten — and he was planning a magical strike that would finish off the AI captain once he was weak enough, allowing him to strike the final blow and take the keep.

"No way in hell," Sam muttered under her breath. She readied her own spell, pouring as much magic and concentration into a flame bolt as she could manage. Then she held the power, watching and waiting from the shadows near the door.

There it was. Thorsten raised his hand to cast his spell.

Sam fired before he could release his magic. The flame bolt spat through the air and exploded against his back. Thorsten cried out in pain and alarm, the force of the blast throwing him from his feet.

Even before he hit the ground Sam was preparing a second bolt. She fired it moments after the first. It slammed into the keep captain's chest. Fire rushed over the AI character. He was blasted backward into the wall, and then sank to the floor in a crumpled ruin.

A gem appeared in Sam's hand, just like the one Harald had acquired when he killed the guard captain. She threw it as hard as she could straight into the hearth-fire. Her aim was true, and it disappeared in a brilliant flash of light.

The green banners on the walls rolled up, and then rolled back down again, but this time they were blue.

Congratulations! You have successfully taken Klaastaad Faste! You are now the Lord of this fort. You earn 1000 Realm Points for this victory.

Congratulations! You have reached level four! You have five attribute points and five skill points to allocate as you choose.

You are now owner of a realm Fort for the blue faction. Please consult the Fort interface to learn more about the abilities this status confers.

She's done it! She'd stolen the kill at the last moment, slipped the win away from Thorsten. Sam laughed aloud, liking how the echoes of her voice filled the hall. Filled *her* hall.

"You bitch," Thorsten shouted from across the room. He was on his feet again, his body a blur of motion. He grabbed a spear, infused it with his magic, and a heartbeat later the weapon was streaking through the air straight at Sam's heart. She raised her shield, hoping the defense would block the blow, but she worried what Thorsten's spell would do. Sam cursed, wishing she had remembered to cast Shield on herself. Now it was too late.

"No hurt Great One!" Gnash was there beside her, shoving Sam out of the way of the missile. The spear which had been intended to kill her struck him instead. The big kobold sank to the ground beside her, clutching the weapon buried in his chest.

39

Sam caught Gnash's body as he crumpled to the floor. She eased him down, trying not to jostle the spear too much. But it had hit something vital inside the kobold. He was bleeding heavily, and gasping for breath. By the time Sam had laid him gently to the floor he was already growing pale.

"Why, Gnash? You don't even like me much!" Sam said.

"You did it for me," Gnash said, and then he died.

Sam let the still body slip from her fingers. Her hands were covered with bright red blood. Her vision was misty with tears. But she rose again, turning back toward Thorsten. The killer laughed.

"Just like a woman, crying over a dead pet. Kobolds are disgusting creatures anyway. Where did you find these things? Have you checked them for fleas yet?" Thorsten called out.

He picked his sword back up from where it had fallen when he fell and then skipped down the stairs toward her. His remaining nine people followed, but slowly. They were looking nervous at the prospect of fighting three dozen angry kobolds.

Sam ignored them all. She looked down at Gnash, his body still and growing cool. Soon it would evaporate, vanishing into mist like everything did after death in this world. But unlike her, Gnash wasn't coming back. He wouldn't respawn in a new body. He was gone.

Something inside her shattered at the idea. She'd been thinking of this place as a game all along. She'd considered the things which happened here worthless, useless, because they weren't real. It was all make believe, after all. But if a being could die, and not come back? That was consequence. That was reality, with all the harshness of the world she'd grown up knowing.

Was Gnash real? He was part of a program, controlled by Artificial Intelligences designed to run similar beings. He talked. He had ideas, and showed emotion. When did something that appeared to be alive begin to matter as much as something that really was alive?

Did the logic, data, and program bytes of an AI-controlled character matter less than hers? After all, everyone uploaded to this place was just logic, data, and program bytes themselves. Which meant it was all real, or none of it was. It all mattered, or none of it did. Including the people. Including herself.

Her mind rebelled against the idea that she was without meaning. But that meant every life had meaning, especially those which were mortal, finite, and would vanish on death.

Sam rose from the dead kobold, her face set. Something had changed for her, and she would need to think about the whole thing a lot more when she had time. Just then, she had an asshole to deal with. She surrounded herself with a shield spell, and readied a ray of frost. It wasn't her strongest attack spell, but it would slow Thorsten and drain some of his stamina. That counted for a lot.

"Just put down the sword, be a nice girl, and *maybe* I won't hurt you...much," Thorsten said.

It wasn't an empty threat. He had hurt her. He'd locked her down under the earth, caved in the entrance and left her there to die. More than once. Those experiences would always linger in her mind. The desperation, the fear that she would be trapped down there forever, dying over and over... she'd carry that for a long time. But she was done running.

"Whoever told you I was a nice girl was dead wrong. And you're an asshole," Sam said.

She released the spell she'd readied. Thorsten had been watching for her to cast another flame bolt, and he tried to dodge sideways to avoid the spell as Sam raised her hand. But the ray of frost moved toward the target much more swiftly than the flame bolt. It lashed out to strike him before he could get out of the way. Rime covered his left arm, spreading over his shoulder and down his flank. He cried out in surprise.

And fear. There was definitely an undertone of fear in his voice. Sam felt a little satisfaction at hearing that.

But he wasn't finished yet. Thorsten recovered quickly from the blow, and smashed his sword hilt into the floor. He'd infused the blow with more magic, and a shockwave blasted out from the spot he struck, carrying through the floor. Sam felt the stones beneath her feet buck a moment before the wave of energy slammed into her shield.

The magic protecting her flared into brilliance, sheltering her from most of the attack. She still lost her footing as the rocks shifted, sending her tumbling to the floor. She hit the ground and rolled — just in time. Thorsten was already moving, striking down with his blade where she'd just fallen. Sam gasped. If she'd been a second slower rolling out of the way...!

She surged back to her feet, swinging her sword at Thorsten's head. He parried. All around them the room had erupted into violence, her kobolds launching themselves at Thorsten's men in a wave. The fight flowed around them, though, leaving them largely untouched. Thorsten was her battle, and both sides seemed ready to respect that.

Her shield was mostly spent blocking Thorsten's last strike. If he hit her with another spell it would be bad news. Sam backpedaled to get a little breathing room and reinforced her shield spell. Thorsten stalked toward her, using the few moments to land a flurry of blows. She blocked the first two, but the third slammed home on her left shoulder. The armor there held, keeping the blade from her skin, but she was going to have one hell of a bruise.

He pressed the attack, one blow after another keeping her off balance. Sam fired a flame bolt at his head, but he ducked off to one side. It careened past him and slammed into one of his other warriors, who fell with a shout.

That left Thorsten off balance for a moment, and Sam tried to press her advantage. She swung her sword at his head. He blocked the blow. She pivoted the blade around his and tried to swing at the other side of his body, but Thorsten predicted the movement and twisted his sword around hers. With a hard flick of his wrist he sent her blade spinning out of her grasp.

"I have no idea where you've found all of this magic," Thorsten panted. "But it will take more than a few tricks to beat me, girl. I've been at this for a long time now. You're still just a novice."

He raised his sword. Sam was defenseless. She had no weapon, no shield... Her spell would block a magical attack, but all she had was her armor against his weapon now. Thorsten hammered a blow down on her. She blocked with her forearm, the armor stopping the blade with a screeching sound of metal on metal. He hit her again, and she felt a bone in her arm shatter with the force of the blow. Sam cried out and fell to her knees. Pain might be reduced in this world, but broken bones still hurt! Thorsten raised his sword to strike her one more time. Sam couldn't block. She didn't have time for a spell.

Gurgle appeared on Thorsten's back as if by magic, clinging to the big man's neck. He growled and bit, clawing at Thorsten's face. Thorsten gave a yelp of surprise but recovered quickly. He grabbed Gurgle and flung him over his shoulder.

The delay was just enough. Sam had readied another ray of frost, and the magic slammed into Thorsten's chest, slowing him as the ice chilled his skin and veins. He grunted with the pain and sudden loss of both health and stamina. The magic had weakened him, but he wasn't done yet.

Sam slipped the fingers of her good hand into her belt, fishing out the little knife Gurgle had given her. She wasn't quite unarmed. She closed quickly with Thorsten, pushing her body up against his, her face just beneath his. The shocked look in his eyes as she drove her knife into his belly just below his ribs was almost worth all the pain he had caused her. Watching the life drain from his eyes, feeling his weight sag against her, and seeing his body slump lifeless to the floor almost took away the weight of the memories and death and sorrow he'd brought her.

Almost.

Around her the battle was finishing. Her kobolds had done their work. Outnumbered, the remaining warriors had fought defensively to keep each other alive. Seeing Thorsten fall, the half dozen remaining fled now, sprinting out the front door of the keep, heading for the walls, for anyplace far from there. Her kobolds gave chase at first, but Sam called them back.

"Let them go," Sam said. "You've all done enough. And we have dead and wounded of our own to care for and mourn."

Sam went to recover her sword, sheathing the weapon. The gates of the fort reappeared. The castle guards were respawning in blue tunics, ready to defend the place against the next attack. The fort was hers now, for as long as she could hold it.

She went to Gnash's body and picked it up, carrying him out into the courtyard. It wasn't enough to let the system simply fade him away like it did every other dead body. She had her kobolds gather wood. She would build a pyre for her dead, and then her warriors would mourn them properly together this evening. Real or not, they had sacrificed and died for her. That made them real enough for her.

40

Sam was standing on the wall keeping watch when Harald came up the steps toward her. She knew he was there, of course. She'd been on guard for hours, alert for any sign of a green counter-attack. Thorsten wouldn't be back until tomorrow, but he'd come after her as well. He would never allow a defeat like this to go uncontested. He'd return, likely with an even greater force.

But Sam knew she'd be ready. She had her kobolds gather up all the weapons from the dead scattered around the fort. But instead of selling them she sent the gear back with a few kobolds to their lair to bring forth more warriors. Only another dozen had answered the call. It seemed there was a limit to what the place might produce for her in terms of warriors. She supposed that made sense; the game wouldn't want one player to gain too great an advantage in that manner. But it still meant that she had forty-two fighters helping her hold the place. Attackers would be hard pressed to win through.

Harald arrived at dusk with his war band. She hadn't

come down to see him. Sam wasn't sure what to say to the man. He hadn't come to help her when she'd needed it. She didn't know why, didn't know if he had even tried, but she couldn't help feeling angry and betrayed.

"You have many guests downstairs. You should be there, helping host," Harald said.

"I'll join them soon enough," Sam said. The sun was setting, the last brilliant yellow beams transforming into red before her eyes. Dawn and dusk were always going to be dangerous times. People were most likely to attack when the light was changing. That had pretty much always been so, and she didn't figure it was much different in this place. But once the sun was down, she would feel a little more secure.

At least until the sun dawned again the next day. Winning the fort had been one thing. Keeping it was going to be entirely another.

"You're Lord of your own fort now," Harald said. "You've earned a spot at the table with myself, Siggund, and other leaders of the faction."

"I got lucky."

"You were lucky," Harald replied. "You were also good. It takes both to come out on top, sometimes."

"What happened? After I left?" Sam asked.

"We held the fort, but it was a close thing. By the time Thorsten got back from chasing you, we'd all but defeated the other enemies," Harald said. "He joined us instead of siding with them. No way to prove that he ever intended anything different."

"Sneaky of him," Sam said.

"But he left at first light. The enemy came soon after he and his men retreated and...we didn't have the forces to hold them back. We were all killed, moved back to the castle,"

Harald paused, and sighed. "I thought Thorsten had killed you. When I didn't find you at the faction castle, I knew something else had happened. But we were trapped. The enemy factions banded together and it took us days to break out."

"Sounds rough," Sam said, her voice dry.

"Not as bad as what I understand you went through."

She turned and arched an eyebrow. "Who's talking?"

"Everyone. Your fame is growing. You have apparently died a thousand times while defeating a legion of undead liches deep inside an ancient underground fortress," Harald said, chuckling. "You've also become a master of sorcery, and can blow walls down with a word and bring back the dead."

Sam smiled through the whole telling, right up until the last. Her grin cracked and fell apart at the final words. "No, not that. I can't bring back those who fell fighting for me."

Harald cocked his head sideways. "I thought you were the girl who didn't think any of this was real?"

"Is it?" she asked.

"You're asking the wrong man," Harald said. He reached out and pinched her arm. Sam yelped, and slapped his hand. "Did that feel real to you?"

"Yes," Sam replied, rubbing her arm.

"That's my take. If it feels real, well... That's good enough for me," Harald said. Then he let his voice grow softer. "Did it feel like real grief when they died for you?"

"Yes," Sam said, her voice cracking.

"Then that should tell you everything you need to know."

They stood a while longer in companionable silence as the sun set, the dark blues of evening overtaking the sky. A squad of kobolds was patrolling the wall. They saluted sharply as they passed Sam. She nodded and smiled back. Enough time had passed. They were safe, at least for tonight. There would be other battles, maybe as soon as tomorrow. But tonight she could rest with the others. Harald seemed to sense the change in her mood and offered his hand to her.

"Shall we return to your hall, Lady Samantha?" Harald asked.

"I think that sounds like a good plan," she replied. "I did want to thank you, by the way."

"Oh?"

"Your gift. The Rune Binding skill. I would never have been able to survive and win through those ruins without it."

"So you did find some magic," Harald said.

"A little." Sam flicked her wrist, and a bolt of flame leapt from her fingers, flying high and arcing away over the wall. Harald whistled at the sight.

"I'm a little jealous. I have my lightning, but no fire spells," he said.

"I have cold and shield magic as well," Sam said. She figured the word was out among her enemies about what spells she could use. Thorsten had seen all her spells in action. She might as well let her allies know what she could do as well.

"We could spend some time working on these together," Harald said. "I'd consider a trade, if you'd like — my lightning rune for one of yours."

"That would be excellent," Sam said. It would expand both of their powers. They were both going to need that edge, in the days to come.

Before they reached the open front doors to the hall,

Harald stopped. Sam halted beside him. He had a strange look on his face.

"What?" she asked.

"All of this — everything you've put yourself through — it's all so you can leave this place, isn't it? You plan to win your way through, so you can leave? Reach the Gods themselves and get a message out?"

"Yeah. I've got a life out there somewhere. I think. Family I never got to say goodbye to, at the very least. I need to *know*, Harald. I need to understand what happened."

He nodded, as if making a decision. "You have my help. Whatever I can do to help you hold this fort, so you can win the Realm Points you need. And...I've been to the realms beyond this one. I swore I was never going back out there again, but this feels like a cause good enough to break that vow. I'll guide you through at least the next realm as well."

"Thanks," Sam said. She didn't know how else to respond. It was an incredible offer. He was one of the strongest warriors in the realm. With his help, her odds of succeeding just went up enormously.

Harald reached out his hand without saying another word. She clasped his arm in the manner she'd seen him and some of his warriors use with each other.

"Good enough then," he said. "Enough of this. Tonight, we feast. And drink!"

They proceeded into the great hall, where a massive throng had gathered. Sam was surprised. She knew many blue faction members had worked their way here, but the sheer number stunned her. Half of her kobolds were inside as well, keeping to themselves at one table and having their own little feast.

"Lady Samantha has arrived in her hall, my friends,"

Harald roared. "We will defend her home as if it were our own."

The cheers shook the building. Samantha's smile came more easily to her at last, because after all she had been through, she finally felt like she had come home.

CONTINUED IN BOOK 2: **RAIDING JOTUNHEIM, available on Amazon today!**

AUTHOR'S NOTES

LitRPG is a fascinating genre. It's fresh, new, and a little weird. Lots of people are getting involved, exploring the confluence of the virtual and the real in one way or another.

This book looks at a special piece of that puzzle. When does the virtual matter just as much as the real? What happens when the players are only virtual themselves, with no meat left in the real world? Do they have rights? Are they still alive, or have those who uploaded themselves to Valhalla Online become merely bytes of data?

These sorts of questions intrigued me, and LitRPG seemed like a wonderful playground in which to explore them. This book is different from my usual "ships fighting in space" fare, but it's been fun — and challenging — to write.

Valhalla Online always held a special place in my heart for a few other reasons. One was that I was a MMORPG guild leader for a long, LONG time. I ran the longest continuously operating "anti-rpk" guild in the world for over a decade: the Defenders of Order.

We were in Asheron's Call, DAOC, Shadowbane, WOW, Conan, Aion, Star Wars KOTOR, Lineage 2, and so many more than I'm forgetting a bunch. It was a good time. I got to see the bonds people forged over games like these. Two of my guild officers married each other. We held multiple in-person guild cons.

The virtual can matter a great deal.

The other reason Valhalla is special to me is that this book, the one you just read, was the book which catapulted me into life as a full-time writer back in 2017. I probably wasn't quite ready for it at the time, but I jumped in anyway after this book took off well. There have been ups and downs since, of course, but it's never been boring.

I always wanted to come back to Valhalla and do one last book. Which is why I've refurbished the first four. I've got one coming out every two weeks, with re-edited and refreshed text, brand new stunning covers, and the fifth book, final in the series, to cap it all off.

I hope you enjoy the books! If you've liked this, please consider leaving a review to let others know it's a good story, and feel free to chat it up with your friends, too. The more readers we have for LitRPG, the stronger the genre will become.

If you've got thoughts, emotions, feelings, or comments about the book, please drop me a line! I can be reached at kevins.studio@gmail.com and would very much love to hear from you!

Kevin

WHERE TO FIND LITRPG AND GAMELIT?

If you're looking for more great stories of the same sort, DO check out the Facebook LitRPG Books page. It's a great group of readers (and a few writers) who are working to push this new genre to the next level.
   https://www.facebook.com/groups/LitRPG.books

To learn more about LitRPG, talk to authors including myself, and just have an awesome time, please join the LitRPG Group.
   https://www.facebook.com/groups/LitRPGGroup/

You can also find more LitRPG goodness here!
   https://www.facebook.com/groups/litrpgforum
   https://www.facebook.com/groups/LitRPGReleases
   https://www.facebook.com/groups/GameLitSociety
   https://www.facebook.com/groups/progressionfictionaddicts

https://www.facebook.com/groups/TheFantasyNation
https://www.facebook.com/groups/LitRPGsociety

A SNEAK PEEK FROM BOOK 2: "RAIDING JOTUNHEIM", AVAILABLE NOW!

CHAPTER 1

More ladders were landing on the ramparts than the defenders could remove. The attackers were going to take the east wall, and there didn't seem to be a damned thing Samantha could do about it. There were just too many of them. The Red, Green, and Black clans had all joined forces for this strike. Her forces had managed to hold Klaastaad Faste for three solid weeks against everything the enemy clans could throw at them individually, but against a massed force like this Sam didn't see how they could prevail.

Over those weeks scores of blue fighters had moved to her keep, using it as a forward base to strike deep into the zones controlled by other teams. Klaastaad was beautifully positioned as a base for deep raids in a variety of directions. That made it a great place to have as a base. It also made it highly desirable. Hell, it was rare for a keep to stay under one team's control for even a few days! That she'd held out so long was part of the problem. All the warriors from the opposing clans saw Klaastaad as a challenge. All of them wanted to be the person who took the fort down. Who took *her* down.

"Samantha, we're losing the wall," Harald said, jogging up to her side.

"I see it," she replied. She was running out of options. Losing the wall meant losing their first real line of defense. They could fight from the inner keep, even hold out there against attack for a while. But it would be a much harder fight.

"You ever seen someone successfully defend if they got pushed back to the inner keep?" she asked Harald.

"No — well, yeah, but not often. Damned rare. You want to retreat?"

"They'll think they won if we do."

"Odds are good they'll be right."

She laughed. "We shouldn't have held out this long. It's been a good run. But I'm not ready to throw in the towel just yet. Sound the retreat."

Harald blew a horn, and troops began pulling back from the walls. They still lost some people as the forces withdrew, but they'd have more left for the defense this way. Sam meant what she's said to Harald. She'd known this day was coming for a while. Her people had already repelled dozens of attacks. It was only a matter of time before someone saw their success as an ant-hill that needed knocking over. But she'd had more than enough time to figure out how to make them pay for every inch.

She nodded to Gurgle, who ordered a squad of her kobolds into action. Short, scaled, and not typically bright, the kobolds were excellent servants and soldiers, but she tended to under-commit them. Once they died, they were gone. They couldn't come back. But they'd turned the tide on many fights. Sam hoped they could do it again today.

They rolled barrels from the walls, hauling them out into the middle of the yard, right in front of the inner keep's doors.

A Red warrior saw them and raced to intercept. He cut down one of the kobolds before Sam could react. Then she was there next to him, slashing in with her blade. He blocked the first strike, but Sam had built up long hours of practice. She twisted her blade around his, circling it and stabbing in. His face turned white as her blade entered just below his ribs. The pain in this world might be less than in the real, but if someone's sword slid into your guts, you surely knew it.

He fell, clutching the wound. Sam ignored him, knowing that her kobolds would finish the job for her. She was more worried about the mixed unit of troops pouring over that wall. She sheathed her sword, calling magic to her hand. A flame bolt shot free from her fingers, knocking on man off the ladder before he could climb over. She fired again, and again, taking down two more of them. But she was trying to plug a tide with a few pebbles.

"Pull back to the keep!" she shouted. "Blue troops, regroup inside!"

They'd already begun the retreat at the sound of Harald's horn. Sam's spells gave them a little breathing room, a gap in the fighting to withdraw cleanly. The troops backed their way down the stairs in good order, keeping the enemy at bay with shield and spear.

Sam fired off two more bolts of magic into the enemy force, mostly to make them shelter behind their own shields. A glance over her shoulder showed her the kobolds were finished with their work. Two of them had already killed the Red soldier she'd left behind. They'd also begun gnawing on his fingers.

She growled at them, and they scurried off, racing ahead of the rest of her troops to get inside the fort. Kobolds; they were useful, but they had the attention span of a small child sometimes. Especially where food was concerned.

And to them, just about anything dead looked like food.

The enemy was pouring over both the East and West walls. Without her troops there to keep them back, the enemy had free reign. They raced down the stairs, hoping to cut off some of her soldiers before they reached safety. They were too slow about it, though. Sam could see all of her people were going to make it inside. She dashed for the doors and ducked inside herself. Harald was already there, a stout wooden beam in his arms. He nodded at her.

"Soon as they're all in," he said.

"I'll be ready."

"There won't be much time," he warned her.

"I said I'd be ready. You going to grouse or fight?" Sam replied, laughing.

"Fight! But I'd rather not fight all of them at once," he replied with a grumble that Sam knew wasn't how he felt.

Harald loved this sort of thing. Much like Sam had grown to love it. Damn, but you felt alive out there! Leading troops, winning victories... Even the wounds and the occasional death were not enough to still the joy it brought her. You always came back, after all.

No, there was only one thing which made her sad these days, and that was the not knowing what was going on with those she'd left behind in the outside world. Sam shoved the thought aside with resilience born from long practice. She needed to concentrate.

The last of her people were on the steps outside the keep, backing up. The enemy was peppering them with arrows, slowing their progress. And a force was down the stairs too, rushing at them. If they were locked in a melee, they'd never get free. She'd lose half of them. They couldn't afford that.

"Harald?" she asked. Sam raised a hand and gathered magic to her.

"On it," he said, grunting as he shifted the heavy beam to his left hand. He raised his right, electricity crackling around it. Then the light flashed around his hand. Like it was answering his call, lightning crashed down from the blue sky, smashing into a cluster of enemy troops, scattering their bodies into the air from the impact.

Sam's own lightning strike hit a moment later, blasting a second enemy formation. It had been enough. The paired spells had them hurting and rattled. Their force was far from broken, but they were coming in a lot slower. They'd bought more than enough time for the last of their Blue troops to get in. Sam slammed the door home behind them, and Harald dropped his beam in place to seal the doors.

"Now for the hard part," Sam said. "Wait for my signal?"

"You sure this is going to work? We've never tried it," Harald asked her.

"No better time for a test, unless you have another plan?"

He just shook his head in answer, a smile bristling behind his white beard. She flashed him a grin of her own and dashed up the stairs toward the upper level of the keep.

READ THE REST TODAY! *Click here: http://mybook.to/valhalla2*

RAIDING JOTUNHEIM
CHAPTER 2

The stairwell was twisted, turning about on itself in a tight spiral. In theory that ought to make it easier to defend. In practice, nobody ever used it that way. It was a silly space the designers had tossed in for virtually no reason at all. To win the fort, all the attackers had to do was break down the doors to the inner keep and then kill the Keep Captain inside. That was an NPC — non-player character — which spawned to help with defense if enemies got past the doors.

He and the other guards which spawned with him were a huge asset, but if they went down, it was all over. A fort's final defense always took place in the main chamber just inside the doors of the inner keep. Nobody was ever going to retreat up the spiral stairs. They were just eye candy.

Until now, anyway. If Sam pulled this off, it was going to spawn a hundred new tricks and tactics around defense. Of course, if it all went sideway they'd have some good chuckles over mugs of mead tomorrow.

She reached the top. The enemy was mostly over the wall now, and the bulk of their force was already in the courtyard. She wanted to wait as long as possible before springing the surprise. Wait too long, though, and the doors would break. Sam glanced at an icon in the lower left corner of her vision, and a small display popped into sight.

Inner Keep Door: 342/500

As she watched, the numbers continued to tick down at an alarming rate. Sam figured she had maybe another thirty seconds before the door went down. She called magic to her hand, readying the spell.

"Is it gonna work?"

The voice from behind her made Sam lose her concentration and miscast the spell. She whirled, angry. It was Jacinda, one of the newer blue recruits. She had taken to following Sam around a lot of the time, which was amusing until it became distracting and dangerous. Like it just had.

"Not now!" Sam yelled. Furious with herself for having lost her concentration, she whirled back toward the enemy force and prepared her magic again. The doors were critically low now. Any moment they'd break, and she had no time to lose.

The flame bolt left her fingers just in time, winging its way toward a target in the center of the mass of enemies. Some of them saw it coming and dove out of the way, which suited her just fine. Better for her that they jump clear. Sam wasn't aiming for a person. Her target was a carefully placed set of objects — the barrels her kobolds had moved.

Flame slammed into the barrels. It was the strongest fire spell Sam could cast. She'd practiced for almost a month now, working to build her magic to the point where it was strong enough to shatter the wood planks of the barrels. The fire bolt struck with enough impact to send chunks of oak in all directions, deadly splinters blasting the enemies masses nearest to the barrels.

The fire also ignited the contents of the barrels as they detonated. They were filled with a light, sticky oil. The highly flammable substance burst into fire, throwing a wave of hot air and burning liquid thirty feet in every direction. Those closest were knocked to the ground by the force of the blast. Burning oil splashed across many who were far enough from the explosion to avoid the shock wave. The oil kept burning even after it struck its victims.

Clothing caught. Men and women ran around, trying to put out their blazes. Some dropped to the ground out of instinct before realizing that burning oil was spreading there, too. In seconds the entire courtyard was a spectacle of fiery death.

The oil began burning itself out rapidly, but the damage was done. Dozens of attackers were dead. Scores more were wounded. Even those who'd been far enough from the explosion to avoid injury seemed shaken and uncertain. They were ready to bolt.

With a roar, Harald led a force from the inner keep into the middle of the demoralized enemy. The doors which had sheltered them burst open and his warriors surged out into the guttering flames, killing the wounded in the courtyard and then pressing on against the rest of their stunned foes. What remained of the enemy force routed as soon as they saw this new threat. There was no command to retreat, no organized withdrawal. They fled in panic, racing back up the stairs, making for their ladders, trying with everything they had to stay a few feet ahead of Harald's bloody axe.

Most of them failed to make it safely back over the wall.

"You did it," Jacinda murmured. She'd kept utterly silent after Sam's rebuke.

"We did," Sam said, heaving a sigh. She felt sorry about using this ruse. It wasn't the way battles were usually fought, here. It might change the nature of the game in this Realm for some time to come. Battles were waged for personal honor or even the honor of a Clan. This sort of war to the knife, win at all costs attitude was rare in Valhalla Online.

But Sam had too much at stake to fail. She needed to hold the keep for just another day or two, and she would have enough Realm Points to leave this place and go to whatever trials awaited her in the next Realm. There were eight, and Harald said she needed to pass into the final one before she would be able to achieve her goal.

More than anything else, Sam wanted contact with the real world outside this virtual one. She had to learn what had happened to her. How she'd come to be here. Whether she was still alive out there or...not. Nothing else mattered, just achieving her goal.

A flash of black caught Sam's attention from the corner of her eye. She turned, catching sight of a man dressed in black garments on the south wall. He had a bow raised, an arrow nocked. The weapon was aimed right at her. Her shield was still below, where it wasn't going to do her much good. Sam dove for cover.

"Look out!" Jacinda shouted. She'd seen the attacker as well. She rushed forward, shoving Sam into the shelter of the battlements.

Sam turned back to order the young woman to get down, but before she could say a word, a black arrow sprouted from Jacinda's chest. There was no blood. Her eyes grew wide. Her mouth shaped an o. But she didn't fall dead to the rooftop as Sam expected.

A black corruption spread from the site the arrow had struck, rushing with furious frenzy over Jacinda's body. In seconds she'd been covered by the stuff. Then she began coming apart like she was made of ash, bits of her body breaking off like black motes, each drifting a short distance on the wind before they too vanished.

The entire process took no more than two breath's time. When it was done, there was no sign Jacinda had ever stood there at all.

DON'T MISS THE REST OF THE ADVENTURE! Grab your copy of RAIDING JOTUNHEIM TODAY!

OTHER BOOKS BY KEVIN MCLAUGHLIN

The Ragnarok Saga (Military SF)
Accord of Fire - Free prequel short story, available only to email list fans!
Book 1 - Accord of Honor
Book 2 - Accord of Mars
Book 3 - Accord of Valor
Book 4 - Ghost Wing
Book 5 - Ghost Squadron
Book 6 - Ghost Fleet (2022)

Valhalla Online Series (A Ragnarok Saga Story)
Book 1 - Valhalla Online
Book 2 - Raiding Jotunheim
Book 3 - Vengeance Over Vanaheim
Book 4 - Hel Hath No Fury
Book 5 - Burn it Down

Lost Planet Warriors (Military SF with light romance)
Book 1 - Desperate Times
Book 2 - Desperate Measures

Dire Straits - Free short story for email list fans!

Adventures of the Starship Satori (Space Opera blended with military SF)

Finding Satori - prequel short story, available only to email list fans!
Book 1 - Ad Astra: Book 2 - Stellar Legacy
Book 3 - Deep Waters
Book 4 - No Plan Survives Contact
Book 5 - Liberty
Book 6 - Satori's Destiny
Book 7 - Ashes of War
Book 8 - Embers of War
Book 9 - Dust and Iron
Book 10 - Clad In Steel
Book 11 - Strange New Worlds
Book 12 - Peace Talks

Blackwell Magic Series (Urban Fantasy)

Book 1 - By Darkness Revealed
Book 2 - Ashes Ascendant
Book 3 - Dead In Winter
Book 4 - Claws That Catch
Book 5 - Darkness Awakes
Book 6 - Spellbinding Entanglements
By A Whisker (short story)
The Raven and the Rose - Free novelette for email list fans!

Dead Brittania Series:

Dead Brittania (short prequel story)
Book 1 - King of the Dead
Book 2 - Queen of Demons

Raven's Heart Series (Urban Fantasy)
Book 1 - Stolen Light
Book 2 - Webs in the Dark
Book 3 - Shades of Moonlight

Other Titles:
Over the Moon (SF romance)
Midnight Visitors (Steampunk Cat short story)
Demon Ex Machina (Steampunk Cat short story)
The Coffee Break Novelist (help for writers!)
You Must Write (Heinlein's rules for writers)

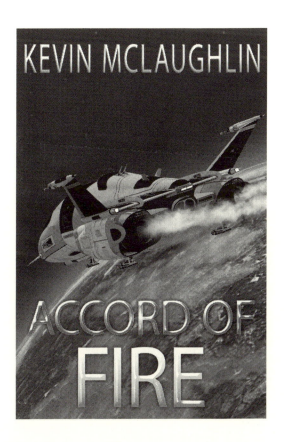

Exclusive free story for fans of Kevin McLaughlin's science fiction!
Find out how the Accord story started... When Captain Nicholas Stein set out to stop one enemy ship, and set in motion events which shaped the course of human history for decades to come.
http://kevinomclaughlin.com/accordoffire/

ABOUT THE AUTHOR

USA Today bestselling author Kevin McLaughlin has written more than three dozen science fiction and fantasy novels, along with more short stories than he can easily count. Kevin can be found most days in downtown Boston, working on the next novel. His bestselling Blackwell Magic fantasy series, Accord science fiction series, Valhalla Online LitRPG series, and the fan-favorite Starship Satori series are ongoing.

I love hearing from readers!

www.kevinomclaughlin.com
kevins.studio@gmail.com

Made in the USA
Middletown, DE
27 December 2021